ROSE ALONE

Sheila Flynn DeCosse

CALEC - TBR Books
New York – Paris

TBR Books is a program of the Center for the Advancement of Languages, Education, and Communities. We publish researchers and practitioners who seek to engage diverse communities on topics related to education, languages, cultural history, and social initiatives.

    CALEC – TBR Books

    750 Lexington Avenue, 9th floor, New York, NY 10022 USA

    198 Avenue de France, 75013 Paris, FRANCE

    www.calec.org | contact@calec.org

    www.tbr-books.org | contact@tbr-books.org

Illustrations: Teresa Lawler

Cover Design: © Nathalie Charles

    ISBN 978-1-636071664 (paperback)

Library of Congress Control Number: 2022933406

PRAISES

After a violent deportation, fourteen-year-old Rose along with thousands of other Acadians. only know that they have lost everything and are under the control of the enemy, the feared and hated English. As the story progresses, neither side trusts the other, often because they don't understand each other, nor speak the other's language. Rose struggles with many problems but in time, she works hard to learn to speak English and finally finds a path forward. It's fine for a reader to learn the facts but all alone, that can be boring to some. Sheila DeCosse found the heart, the passion, the feelings of this story. That's what draws people in.

—Jean Doris LeBlanc, Acadian historian-genealogist, retired teacher

Sheila Flynn DeCosse captures the mood of the era of the French and Indian War through the eyes and ears of young Rose, one of over 6000 Acadians who were forced to leave their homes and farms in Nova Scotia, by the English in 1755. By carefully reconstructing the sights and sounds of an environment over 250 years ago, the author becomes Rose, a displaced Acadian child, separated from her family and often viewed as the enemy amongst many of the American colonists she has been forced to shelter with. This is a very touching tale that seems so appropriate for the present time. With ethnicity and immigration problems in the forefront of world news, this story of the plight of the Acadians, seen through Rose, reminds every

teenage reader, that with the right attitude, there can be a happy ending.
—Richard I Barons, Chief Curator, East Hampton Historical Society

An entertaining and educational story of an Acadian girl caught in perilous times in colonial East Hampton, New York as she struggles to find her lost family and settle in a new land.
—Barbara Strong Borsack
Descendant of early East Hampton settlers.

ROSE ALONE is a compelling story of Acadian settlers in North America caught between three cultures-French, English and Mi'kmaq- as they struggle to keep their own independence during the French and Indian War. Sheila Flynn DeCosse makes history come alive for young readers.
—David Kuchta, Ph.D., independent historian

ROSE ALONE is a rich and engrossing novel that illuminates an overlooked but worthy pocket of history. With an eye for vivid detail and a deft feel for the story's unique setting, author, Sheila DeCosse draws readers into a captivating story that resonates long after the final page has been read.
—Elizabeth Doyle Carey, author

DEDICATION

Jacqueline Henriette Pace

In memory of Madame as we called her; this dedicated teacher put up with the inattention of our American high school class. She was a former girlhood spy for the French Resistance. A kind, scholarly young woman when we knew her, she was devoted to transmitting the French language and literature and had us reading Molière and Racine as well as studying French grammar. My regret is profound that I did not continue higher-level French studies, with my only excuse, that no later teacher could compare to her.

ACKNOWLEDGEMENTS

There are many to thank! My son David E DeCosse, first told me about the Acadians in East Hampton in colonial times. Dorothy T. King, Head of Collections at the Long Island Collection of the East Hampton, New York Library, first guided my research. David Kuchta, editor-historian, first recognized worth in, and edited my early texts. Appreciation by Richard Barons, emeritus Executive Director of The East Hampton Historical Society, gave me the confidence to pursue a relatively unknown Long Island historical subject. Jean Doris Le Blanc, Acadian teacher, read early stages of my manuscript and checked for cultural and grammatical errors. East Hampton Star former associate editor, Joanne Pilgrim copyedited carefully. Children's book guru, Editor Emma D. Dryden, straightened out the plot lines. Andrea Meyer, current Head of Collections at The Long Island Collection of the East Hampton Library provided additional sources for colonial information. Jula DeCosse, my granddaughter, copy edited and wrote copy. The legendary writing class of Margaret Bunny Gabel at the New School and the work of the accomplished authors in her class, showed me what it takes to be a children's book author. Then, Elizabeth Doyle Carey, author and editor, nearly published my book, which gave me hope. The enthusiasm of Daisy Eckman, my first East Hampton young reader, who kept asking for the next chapter, and the determination of religious Sister Beatrice Brennan,

RSCJ, then living in Louisiana, who personally toured me around to Acadian "joints" and houses, raised my spirits. The fine artist, Teresa Lawler, after studying the manuscript, furnished graceful illustrations. Elisabeth Margaret Mclaughlin, tamed my unruly Word skills into readable English and Emma Rodriquez checked all points, French, English, and interior layout, with great care.

In a special acknowledgment category, however, are these "last shall be first" individuals. Barbara Le Blanc, Université Sainte-Anne-Nova Scotia Scholar of Language, and guardian of national historic sites, who patiently guided me to Acadian information, Jane F. Ross, my personal friend and author educator at the Alliance Française in New York City, who made the editorial contact and copy read with care and Fabrice Jaumont, Editor and Language Scholar, who accepted my book for the international press, TBR Books.

To the members of my Bunny Gabel writing critique group, an outgrowth of her legendary class, I send my special thanks for their patience, skill, and wisdom in commenting on my endless drafts. Following our intrepid leader, Karen DelleCava, they are: Susan Amesse, Barbara Baker, Steven Alan Boyar, Selene Castrovilla, Alice Golin, Emily Goodman, Michelle Granger, Sherry Koplan, Patricia Lakin, Sandy Landsman, Laurent Linn, Arlene Mark, Kathy Bieger Roche, Michelle de Savigny, Vicki Shiefman, Seta Toroyan and Paricia Weissner.

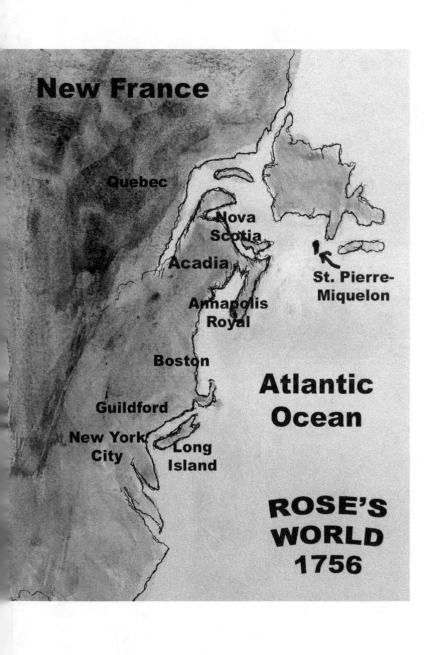

TABLE OF CONTENTS

"The Governor of New York decreed that these newly arrived French Neutrals, lately from Acadia, are dangerous enemies in our midst. They refused to honor the British Crown and may try to start a battle among us for the French cause. These people could be dangerous. Beware of them. They and their Indian allies have killed many of our people."

(When the Acadian ship arrived in New York City)

From The Pennsylvania Gazette, September 4, 1755, published. Halifax.

HALIFAX CANADA: August 9, 1755.

"We are now upon a great and noble Scheme of sending the neutral French out of this Province, who have always been our secret enemies, and have encouraged our Savages to cut our Throats. If we effect their expulsion, it will be one of the greatest Things that ever the English did in America; for by all the accounts, that Part of the Country they possess is as good Land as any in the World. I case therefore we could get some good English farmers in their Room, this Province would abound with all Kind of Provisions."

CHAPTER ONE

BEWARE THE ENGLISH

"We are lost," Papa said. I don't think he meant that we are lost on this road in Acadia. I think he means we have lost hope. Whatever, the chill in my heart deepens.

I am Rose, a dark-eyed, black-haired, Acadian girl of fourteen years of age. Listen to me. I have a tale to tell.

Under my winter party clothes, my red and black striped skirt, my shawl, my black vest, and wool stockings, my heart sinks into a cold, black hole. The dancing at the wedding may warm my legs up, but the ice in my heart will remain.

These are dangerous days.

CLUNK, CLUNK, BAM. The wooden wheels on our red cart shift from one frozen road rut to another; Maman and I, sitting together on the front bench, jounce and bump as well: our insides jolting against our ribs. In the hay in the back of our wagon, my little brother and sister, Jacques and Madeleine, are fast asleep. Their ribbon-trimmed feast-day clothes peek out from under the hay.

"Maman, will Auntie Françoise and Marie Josèphe be there?" I ask.

Maman turns to me, and I see her nut-brown eyes, warm and concerned at the same time. "Yes, I think so," she says. She shakes her head the way she does when she is sad about the way one of us children, acts.

"You were fortunate that I let you come today, Rose," Maman says. "I still cannot believe that last night you slid on the ice on the *rivière* 'til moonrise. You must have lost your senses."

"I did, Maman. I was visiting Marie Josèphe, and we forgot the time. Earlier, we had such fun at her friend's house making apple tarts for *Noël*."

"I might have left you home to think about what you did," Maman sighs. "But Papa wanted you to come. He said," We must enjoy our families now. Who knows? Who knows?"

Suddenly, I remember my father's words: He told me that there are many English soldiers in town, shipped up to Acadia from Massachusetts. We've heard that they're here to conquer the French Fort, Beauséjour.

I'm an Acadian girl that speaks French, but we are not French. And we want no trouble with the English. Our Acadian ancestors came from France to this land on the Northeast Atlantic shore some hundred and fifty years

ago. They created a new community here in northeast
America and settled our own villages, and built dykes to
hold back sea tides and make fertile land. They called our
region, Acadia, because that means a fertile land of peace.

But Papa says that when the Acadian elders met with the English Governor here, the meetings were not peaceful. That indeed is bad news.

Maman's voice cheers me up. "Rose, enjoy yourself today. Weddings are a time for joy, especially for us Acadians. Yes?"

"Yes, Maman." I am so thankful that she is not still angry with me about our ice sliding.

I raise my voice, "Under my shawl, I am wearing the new chemise I wove. Marie Josèphe says that the low neck is a bit daring but as long as my elbows are covered, *Père* Charles will not object."

Maman laughs her big jolly relaxed laugh. "*Père* Charles may not object. But Papa may. He sometimes is more holy than the Pope, I think!" She looks at me with a smile, "If you pull your neck scarf down just a little, no-one will notice."

"Ah, Maman, you're so clever." We exchange sly glances and chuckle together.

"That is true," I say quietly. "But Papa seems to have much on his mind these days. Maybe he will not notice at all."

"If it is anything to do with his children, Rose, he will notice," Maman says.

"Here, why don't you drive the ox? My hands are freezing." She pulls the ox to a stop. We shift places in the wagon. The ice floes in the river crash and bang against each other and just the sound makes me feel colder.

I raise my voice so Maman and I can hear each other. "Yesterday, I heard Papa say, "French and English soldiers are fighting in America in the Ohio Territory, but we Acadians do not want to fight at all!'

Maman sighed, "Papa may say that. But your brother Pierre wants to fight against the English and drive them all out of Acadia." Maman half-smiles at me, "There is a time to be brave," she sighs. "But why not just try to get along with the English as we have for years." She shrugs her shoulders and sinks into silence.

Last night in the moonlight, I saw Papa swing up on Plume, our white stallion. He never came home. My guess is that Papa and Pierre went to a meeting about dealing with the English,

Pierre is my older brother. I am fourteen, and he is seventeen, only three years older than I. Yet, it seems as though that Papa considers him almost an elder. Papa speaks frankly to him about problems with the British.

Pierre always makes sure that I know Papa consults with him. So, Pierre thinks that he is smarter than I am and that gives him an excuse to give me orders. Ah hah!

I'm just as smart as Pierre and I do not like him telling me what to do!

"Maman," I say, "I hope Papa talks to me as well as to Pierre in these days. I will tell them that I know a lot about the native peoples, the Mi'kmaq who lived here before us."

Maman's eyes fix on mine, "*C'est vrai, Rose, ma fille.* You are smart enough. Let's get ready for the wedding!"

"*D'accord*! I love going to weddings," I say. "The pies, the music, the dancing." I dream on. "I hope André will be there," I finish. Maman turns and smiles at me.

CHAPTER TWO

THE WEDDING

A mile later, I steer the oxen over an icy, slippery road towards the Farm on a bluff over the river. Neat houses and barns are arranged around a large, cleared field. Racing children and barking dogs run and slide across the icy ground. Several oxcarts before us are unloading baskets and older aunties wrapped in blankets for the chill. I hear the papas' deep voices calling to their children.

Marie Josèphe, my best girl friend, rushes up as we tie up our ox to a sturdy hitching post. "We were here first!" she announces. "I'm ready for the dancing," she teases as she hops from foot to foot in her soft deerskin moccasins, traded from our native friends, the Mi'kmaq peoples.

I look at the shoes decorated with beads, pine needles and shells and bang my clunky wooden shoes against the cart floor in frustration.

"We still wear our wooden sabots and Maman has put our moccasins, wrapped in a cloth, in a basket. I hope the apple tarts we brought for the party are not too close!"

I smile at Marie Josèphe. "Did you learn any gossip about new betrothals, so we can go to another fête?"

Marie Josèphe's broad red-cheeked face crinkles with worry, making her look old, almost like my *bonne-maman*.

"No, Rose. My Papa left before us to go to a meeting near the English headquarters in Annapolis Royal. I thought that he'd be here early to set up the tables for the wedding feast. Do you know anything about the meeting?"

I suddenly remember the strange look that Papa had in his eyes when he spoke to me last night, "Only that my Papa worries about the English. Their leader, Governor Charles Lawrence, keeps insisting that we Acadians promise to fight alongside his English soldiers if a French force should attack this place."

"We'll never fight against the French. Our ancestors came from France," Marie Josèphe says, and we both stamp the ground to end that idea.

"*Vrai!*" we both raise our hands and wave them about as if we had ribbons to wave.

"Yes, today, let's have some fun," I dance a bit in my soft moccasins.

Maman pulls her heavy sealskin furs closer around her shoulders. "Please help me with the food baskets to the barn," she says to us both. To me, she says quietly. "We may have to leave the fête early. Papa warned me. Let me know where you are after supper."

"*Oui, Maman,*" I say, my voice gentle. I so much want in my heart to help Maman. '*Ma petite Cécile*' as Papa calls her, seldom loses her warm, friendly ways.

But now, something is worrying her. "After the dancing I will gather the little ones from the high hay lofts," I tell Maman. "Madeleine is sure that she will find a kitten up there, just like Marie-Thérèse's little sister did at the last fête."

As we set out to the barn, I see our two men, Papa Charles and older brother Pierre, ambling their way across the field chatting with friends and waving to us.

Perhaps all the trouble is settled. When Papa arrives with Pierre, they say nothing about problems. They lift the heaviest baskets of food, and Maman takes the hands of our little ones: with their clothes decorated with pretty ribbons, they are so excited to come to the wedding party.

I look about for my special young man friend, André. But then another girlfriend runs up to Marie Josèphe and me. We three girls stroll arm in arm across the packed snow, chatting with all our friends from our village, Belle Isle.

Suddenly, we see that our priest is calling for attention. He stands on a wagon. "Let us pray," he begins, "that our young couple today will be blessed in their marriage. Let us give thanks for our good harvest this fall, and may His blessings fall upon us like the dew from God's hand."

"Amen," we all say. And again, I cast my eyes about for André. Perhaps his English Papa made him work in his shop in Annapolis Royal.

Mon petit frère Jacques is tugging my hand. "Let's eat!" he begs. I send him off to find Maman at the food tables. Mmm! I see *le jambon* and *les poisons* and *des petits gâteaux*, no-one here will be hungry!

And then I see my favorite, André. He stands a bit away from the crowd, on the bluff, looking downriver to Annapolis Royal. I've slowly learned that André is not quite comfortable with all us Acadians. When we met in his Papa's shop in the village, I thought he was Acadian as he looks like his Maman, who is Acadian. But he is only half-so. André's skin and black hair are like his Acadian mother's, Nathalie. But his eyes are blue. His father is English, and so they live a more English life in the village of Annapolis Royal: it is better for his father's trade with British customers.

As I walk over to speak to André, I think of asking him if there is any gossip in the village, he's seventeen and talks to the men who visit their shop. But then I see full sailed ships and sloops sailing into the harbor. It is late in the year for such big ships to arrive here. And to see so many ships at one time is very strange.

André lightly takes my hand, and I forget what I was going to ask...

"I hear the singers and harp players," he says with a smile. "Let's go and join them."

"Ah, yes, I want to hear you sing." We hold hands as we tramp over the snow and as we come into the barn, so, I see the aunties nodding and smiling.

The singers wave to André. He squeezes my hand, leaves me and after a moment, he stands alone and sings. He does not look at me. He does not have to. His voice is as clear and pure as a thrush in the forest. It touches my heart and soul. A still falls over the crowd and then they tease and applaud him. And the Acadian aunties... I see them... cluck and chatter and smile and look at me. There are few secrets among us now.

Later that night, after the dinner and dancing, a full moon gleams over the snow on the mountain ridges and the ice floes grumble in the river beside the road. Papa drives and Maman sleeps, slumped against him. Pierre expertly rides our stallion, and I cuddle in the back of the cart with the little ones in the straw under the beaver skins.

When we reach home, we all fall into beds filled with furs and quilts. The next day is a Sunday so we must rise early and leave in our cart for church. I breathe a prayer that all will be well and fall, then fall sound asleep.

CHAPTER THREE

MAKING FRICOT

Alone. How strange it is. But today I like it. This morning, it was bright and cold when Maman, Papa, Jacques, and Madeleine piled into the ox cart to go to *Église St- Jean-Baptiste*. They always pray that all of us Acadians stay safe in our Acadian homes and lands.

I stood at the door for a few minutes, watching them go down the road to Annapolis Royal. Another house nearby has light flickering in the windows. We here in Belle Isle are church goers and I see carts filled with large families coming down the road. One family I see has two or even three wagons hitched up to take all their children and aunties to church. I watch them another minute as they pass the cold, leafless apple orchards and then turn the corner out of sight.

My throat is red-sore so Maman said I could stay home. She knows I have my dog, *Gardien* to protect me. He is fierce and can scare away wolves when watching the cattle. And now, in our snug house, the fire glows and the chicken, onions and potatoes await the salt pork. I am the

Maman. Now, if only my fricot turns out one-half as good as my Maman's!

Knock, knock, knock! Everyone is gone, who could that be? I take my wooden sabot off my foot, and hold it above my shoulder.

"Who's there?" my voice trembles. I have to be careful.

"*Bonjour!*" calls André's strong voice, "Don't be afraid. Open the door, Rosalie!"

He speaks in French because I do.

"Maybe I will not," I say, knowing he'll be laughing at my tricks. Holding my wooden shoe in a threatening pose, I open the door. And there he is, tall and slender, with snow covering his sealskin coat and cap. His horse, stomping, and blowing, draped in snow, stands behind him.

He comes inside, dripping snow and gives me a hug. Not that I don't want one, but he's cold as an icicle. "Wait," I say, "Put the horse in the barn first, then hurry back." He turns and stomps to the horse, leads him to the barn, and with a light knock, he is back.

"André, but why have you come?"

"Can we talk for a minute?"

"*Oui*, yes. Here's a knife, you can peel onions for the fricot while I chop up the chicken. And we can talk."

"Rose? Not now!"

"It'll only be a minute."

"Rose, me, cooking! I have important, *très* important things to talk about, and you hand me an onion!"

"Maman asks Papa to help her, now that he can't do much field work anymore. Not often," I admit, "or he'd revolt."

"As do I!" André says. "But just this once. And, while we work, you must listen with the ears of your heart to what I have to say."

"But of course, *Monsieur*." I catch the solemn tone of his voice. This is serious.

The fire snaps and throws out hot embers. For a few moments, we work in silence, first dropping the cut chicken into a pot to fry in bear fat, then the onions. When we drop in the last piece, André grabs a cloth, wipes his hands, and lays a hand on my arm. I look up, surprised, and pull the iron pot to the side of the hearth.

"You must listen now, Rose, for I have bad news, terrible news. And we need to know what to do. The English Commandant in Annapolis Royal, Major John Handfield, told Papa about it. The English plan to arrest all Acadians in this area, load them on ships, and send them to English colonies in America or French holdings overseas!"

Strong as I am, a chill rushes through me. I lift my head to look into André's eyes. "I cannot believe it! The officer... we have known Handfield for years, he would do this to us?"

"Yes, much as he detests the order, he has to carry it out. His orders came from the office of His Excellency, Governor Charles Lawrence in Halifax. The ships to carry Acadians away lie waiting in the harbor of Annapolis Royal."

André wipes his arm across his eyes, which water from the onions. "*C'est incroyable*," he says. "I, too, can hardly believe this. It sounds unbelievable, but it's true. It's true for you, your whole family…all Acadians."

"How can he do such a thing! "I stammer. "Pierre has a gun. When last June the English ordered all Acadians to turn in their guns, he and a few others hid their guns in the forest. He and others can fight back."

"The English have two thousand soldiers in the area. They wouldn't have a chance."

"What can we Acadians do?"

"Even if you and others could find passage to get away on a sloop, there is no hope for protection at the French Fort Louisbourg. English ships are blockading the harbor there. Papa says that in his store, he has heard from angry English soldiers that a few wily Acadians have hidden small boats on the shores of la Baie de Fundy and sailed to freedom in New Brunswick, to St John's River. Maybe others have run into the woods to seek help from the Mi'kmaq. I'm not sure," André says.

"Papa could never make it across the fields, woods and water. His weakness has grown worse this past year. He collapsed with chest pain working on the dykes. Often, his heart pounds in his chest; he's not strong."

Looking at André, I slowly reason out, "You're half-English, and your Papa is a shop-keeper in your English village, so whatever happens, you are safe, especially since your English Papa is well liked by the English people in Annapolis Royal..."

"Yes, true, but do you forget...my Maman is Acadian?"

"*Oh, mon Dieu*, that's true."

"That's why I'm here, Rose. I came to ask you if you will escape with me and my Maman, before Handfield starts his arrests."

"Oh, André!" Heat rises to my cheeks, "*Merci*..." As I look at him, I try to be calm. "*Merci*, André, are you sure?" I pull myself up to my full fourteen-year-old height, which is not very tall. "I've not yet finished weaving my wedding sheet."

Heat rises to my cheeks thinking about actually being married. "But even though I'm young, still, André I want to be with you." Then, suddenly I start to shake, and my words tumble out, my heart trembles, "And you're but seventeen…."

My voice sinks low for I am overcome by the sudden decisions ahead of me.

Pulling my long black hair over my face a little, to hide the few tears that slide down my face, I drop my head. André and I have easily talked about pledging love to each other before this, but then we were thinking about after our vows were proclaimed and our families were about us.

Fear clouds my mind, and my feelings are all mixed up.

"Rose," André says softly, "this is a mountain of hopes and fears to dump in your lap. But I don't want to lose you."

"André, are you sure you want this," I say softly.

"Rose, I wouldn't have ridden through the storm this day, unless I was," he stands in front of me, his deep blue eyes steady and speaks quietly. "We must leave soon or our whole life may never be the same. People in the village say that none of the Acadians will know where he or she will be sent, but it probably will be to English colonies or even to France."

"But our dear home, our barn, our wheat fields that we claimed from the salt marshes, they belong to us!"

André frowns, "Not anymore! The English want these very farms for their own settlers."

"They cannot just take them!"

"They can, with all the soldiers they have here now."

"It's stealing! Père Guillaume will stop them."

"He's been shipped back to France..." André shakes his head.

"Here's what I think now, Rosalie. You and I could leave on my father's sloop, in a day or so, with my Acadian mother. The English troops would most likely let us go because my father is English, and he would pay them. We'll sail to Boston where Papa has friends in the Port... He has traded there for years. We'll ask them to hide us in the countryside on an isolated farm. If in time, you truly wish so, we could be married. But we must leave before..."

As André talks, I try to quiet the fears and joys that race around my heart... I try to remember what Papa told me about only speaking when I am calm. But, instead, I blurt out, "You'll never make it! Any captain that could let you though will be afraid of Handfield or Lawrence."

André's chin jerks up as if he's been hit in the stomach, "Rose! You don't know that! It's a better hope for you to come with us, than to be loaded onto the English ships and sailed off to no-one knows where."

"Oh, André, I don't know what I'm talking about. I lost my head and spoke out. André, I'm scared for us all. I love you but I love my family so much. Papa's heart might not stand the shock if I leave with you... And I think I love you but we are young yet and..." He reaches across the table to hold my hands in his.

"I don't know what to do," I whisper.

"Rose, this is the moment to decide," he says gently.

"I cannot leave them, André. Pierre may be captured by the English troops. Although my parents still work hard, Papa is weak and Maman is tired out. And we have the two little ones to care for; Jacques is six and Madeleine only four years. I take care of them most of the time. I am the only strong one left at home."

Standing then I look at my André. His dark eyes hold mine in his as I struggle with the hopes, cares, and pictures we both have had, of us growing together as a family. "You know I want to be with you, but I just cannot leave them, now."

"I believe you, Rose. I know, I know. It is a daring request. But this is a desperate time. I so want to rescue you from the cruelty of the English soldiers. Here in Annapolis Royal, there are stories that the English soldiers have killed some of your people and hidden away their bodies. The ships in the harbor may take you away from me forever. Please know Rose, even now, when we are young, I think of our later life together, perhaps our children… I care deeply for you."

André gently reaches out and takes both of my hands into his. His are warm but mine are cold. André carefully places one of his hands over and one undermine and holds them against his heart.

"Rose, I understand that you want to protect your own family. God bless and keep you, dear one for that."
"But now I must go," he says. "I must get home and decide what my Maman and I should take on our journey. Even for me, getting back to the village is dangerous. The soldiers around here are angry that some of your people have already gotten away from them. They're disobeying orders and stopping people to rob them. My mother hoped you would agree and come with us. But as mothers are, "he smiles," as mother's do, she also worries about me."

"The road from Belle Isle to home is like an ice pond tonight. I must go back to Annapolis Royal and prepare to leave with her. And you, too, Rosalie, must prepare your family: to be ready to leave very soon." He holds me to him and kisses me for a brief moment.

Then he steps to the door, throws on his wet furs and wrenches the door open. As he steps out, he looks back at me, holds my eyes in his and then, the door twists out of his grasp and slams.

CHAPTER FOUR

BRINGING THE NEWS

I hardly sleep, and in the light-morning, I hear Papa up after the cock crows. He walks by my bed-in-the-wall dressed in his wool pants and shirt, with fur skins draped over his shoulders and his wooden shoes clumping on the floor.

I wonder where he is going so early. Out-the-door he goes, it's cold outside, the air from the open door hits my face. But his stocky body seems to have its own heat and very soon, he's back. His warm brown eyes smile at me as he walks by my bed holding a bundle of split wood to his chest.

I don't want to get up except that I know that I have to, to give Papa the news André brought last night. "*Papa*," I say low. Then, yanking a blanket around myself, I jump out of my warm space. I have to move fast, or I'll let myself fall back into the nest of coverlets and furs in the bed-in-the-wall I share with Madeleine.

I'm never as warm as Papa because I'm skinny still, even though I eat lots of Maman's meat-pies, fricot and *briques blanches*. He always teases me that I haven't yet grown to look like a sturdy Acadian woman. But maybe I'll stay this way, Maman is Papa's second wife, my Maman, Françoise, died in my childbirth. I hear that she was of strong build. But Maman Cécile is *petite*, and she's as sturdy as many of the other women. Maybe I'll grow strong, wiry and tough, like her and my Papa, before he got sick.

Papa cracks small dry branches for kindling and then throws a big log on the fire. Scuffing on bare feet over the cold floor, I scare Papa as he bends low over the fire.

"Papa! While you and the family were at church, André came here yesterday!"

He stops poking the fire, turns to me and smiles. "Well, Rose, your friend comes here often, it's good that he came."

"Papa, he had to come," my voice suddenly trembles, "Papa, he had horrible news and he asked me a big question."

"You're shaking Rose, come sit near me, by the fire," he gently pulls me beside him, and I stare at the crackling flames, feel their warmth, and know I have to speak. I tense my fingers tight into my palms hands together and look at Papa. His tanned face seems to have more wrinkles around his brown eyes. He runs his fingers through his beard as he often does when he thinks about a problem.

I feel a tear sliding down my face. "First, the worst..."

"You're shaking, daughter. What's the matter? Is he hurt?"

"André told me that English soldiers under orders from Governor Lawrence will soon arrest all of us Acadians here in Belle Isle and living near Annapolis Royal and sail us away to no-one knows where! André's Papa is English and English friends of his in Annapolis Royal town told him."

Papa slumps. He breathes deeply. Suddenly, his sturdy frame seems to shrink. He looks at me, his eyes tearing, "Rose, Are you sure? I had heard that Lawrence got very angry with our Acadian men who said they would only sign the oath of allegiance to England if they could also get a promise that they would not be forced to fight against the French Army. I know that the English fear us helping the French. But ...Oh my G—! How can they do this! What else did André say?"

This was the part of André's news that tore my heart most and at first, I couldn't speak. I looked down and composed myself and then raised my eyes to Papa's. "Papa, he asked me to leave Acadia with him and his Acadian mother. His English father could arrange it."

Papa's eyes are clear now. He pulls me to his chest and hugs me tight, then sits back and gently asks, "And what did you tell him?"

"Papa, I was all mixed up in my head and heart. I took time and prayed and finally told him, "I feel I'm too young. I can't leave my family now. They need me.'"

Shaking his head, Papa said, "My dear child, I'm not sure that you followed your own heart."

CHAPTER FIVE

FRENCH NEUTRALS

Papa mutters in a soft voice, "This is our end; what can we do, to leave our own farm that we carved from the woods and leave our dyked salt flats... forever? It cannot be!"

He looks up and tells me in a clear voice, "Governor Lawrence is a bad person. Even some of the English dislike him. Years ago, we accepted an oath of allegiance to England offered to us by the then Governor Richard Philipps, in the name of the British Crown, which said that we Acadians should pledge allegiance to England but that in the event of war that we Acadians could be neutral, especially not fight against any French forces and the agreement also gave us the right to practice our Catholic religion. It was then we became known as the French Neutrals.

But since then, there have been doubts that the oath was valid. Now Governor Lawrence will not let us use the old oath of allegiance to England. He probably fears that we, being so numerous, will ally with the natives and the French and overcome his English colony…"

Papa's voice wavers. He drops his head in his hands. "May God protect us." He drops his head lower. "We are lost."

"Papa," I whisper, but dare say no more, for his shoulders are shaking and great strong Papa weeps like a forsaken child.

"Does Maman know?"

"She knows Papa. It was so busy last night when you all came in from church. And I didn't want to scare the little ones. Then you went to the barn to feed the cow, came back and while I heard Jacques' prayers, you fell asleep. I told Maman last night after you fell asleep that we should wait to tell you. But what can we do Papa? This is terrible news. How can we stop them? Where's brother Pierre?"

"Out on patrol; there are so many English soldiers wandering about since after they captured Fort Beauséjour … I don't know where he is. I don't know." Papa's body shakes, sitting on the bench. He is bent over with his head in his hands. He is silent.

Outside, the shutters creak in the wind, the geese cry as they fly high overhead. I hear the hiss and snap of the fire. These are all part of my life.

OH how I want to stay here! We can't be made to move, just like this! They promised us we could live here as French neutrals, and live as we wish.

Maman's fresh curtains hang at the windows, her colorful rag rugs lie on the floor. Our rough table was made by Papa when he was in strength and could handle the weight of the wide-cut boards. We cannot leave here! This is our home.

Maman quietly comes and sits with us. "Our families, our church. We may lose all of them." She lunges towards Papa and hugs him, nearly knocking him from the bench.

"Charles, what can we do?"

CRASH! CRACK! Our door! What is happening? I'm too scared to move.

BANG! Our door, something attacks us like a charging bull. A musket sound explodes it seems like in our house. My dog *Gardien*, howls in fright. Little Madeleine screams. More loud voices and shouts. "OPEN! OPEN!"

Could it be? Are the English soldiers here?

"*Qui est là?*" Papa mutters, not opening the door.

"OPEN!" a rough voice calls in English, again.

Still Papa stands without moving.

Jacques runs and peeks out the little glass window near the door. "Papa, it's English soldiers," he whispers.

"In the name of His Majesty, King George the Second, open the door!" BOOM!

What might be a musket butt, hits the door, and it splinters. CRACK...

Slowly, Papa walks a few steps and lifts the heavy plank that secures the door closed. The door crashes open, bangs back hard against the wall.

A uniformed English officer stomps into the room. He pauses to smooth down the lace on the lapel of his jacket. Then he thumps his gun on the floor in front of Papa.

I stand beside Papa and glare at the officer. The fat-swine waves to a young soldier to come inside and stand beside him; the boy drops the papers he carries and bends to grasp them, then he stands up and clicks his heels.

The young soldier bellows mixed-up French words to us all. Maman cries out, "*Attendez*! We don't understand!"

The boy looks at the officer who frowns and stamps his gun on the floor again and shouts, "*Encore*!"

The boy starts again. Now he is scared, and his voice drops as he reads. Papa must understand because he has collapsed on the bench. He rubs drops of water away from his forehead and his mouth drops open.

The young soldier reads again. We all this time hear, "By order of Governor Charles Lawrence, now in command of the land of Nova Scotia, it is decreed that you and all your Acadian people must leave this land forever. You must leave this house taking with you only your money and such things as will be necessary for a voyage by ship."

"Oh!" Papa staggers. Maman, rushes over to the hearth, grabs a bottle of spruce beer and brings it to Papa, who takes a gulp. I hold Papa's arm and help him sit upright.

Behind me, my little sister Madeleine, seeing Maman and Papa so upset, wails loud shrieks, sucking in her breath in gasps.

"Be ready!" the officer-soldier grunts. I strain to hold Papa's chest upright. He's leaning on me and his weight's very heavy.

The soldier's rough commands hit me like blows to my body. I sway but still stay beside Papa. My little sister, Madeleine, screams louder and then my brave little brother, Jacques, grabs a fire-tool and and seeing that this young soldier has scared his Papa, rushes towards him.

Brave as Jacques is, Maman jumps up and catches him and hauls him back from what might be a hard cuff from the officer.

"Be ready!" the soldier-brute says. "We'll be back. Be ready!" and he stomps out of the door, leaving it wide open to the blowing snow outside.

"What can we do, Maman, Papa? What can we do?" Frantic words fly out of my mouth.

"Rose, sit down here with Maman and me." Papa grabs my hand in his, still a solid and warm grasp. I sit down on a little bench, across the table from the two of them, my two dear parents. Papa's eyes are clear now. "This is Lawrence's doing… He will have no mercy. This must be why he ordered all Acadians to give up their guns.

Maman and Papa look at me, their faces lined with tears. Maman raises her right hand and makes a cross from her forehead to her heart, and her two shoulders, then puts her open palms together. "We must pray, and plan," she says. "We have… no choice.".

She takes a deep breath, drops her eyes and seems to be within herself until she speaks, and we join, in to pray the Our Father. Putting her hand on the table to steady herself, she walks to the hearth to fetch the risen bread loaf and picks it up to bake in our bread oven.

As she sits down at the table again, a voice from outside faintly calls, *"Hallo, c'est moi, Marie Josèphe!"* Papa opens the door quickly. There stands my best friend, Marie Josèphe.

She is a little older than I but the same age as my brother Pierre, seventeen. We're just about opposite in appearance, with me a scrawny little person and her, a sturdy near woman whose bellowing laugh is nearly as loud as Pierre's.

Many *canoës* rides we've had together on La Rivière Dauphin, and many hours spent helping each other at our two houses, working in the garden, helping to, ugh, butcher hogs, and knitting socks for our Papa's. But better: many hours we've danced at our Acadian weddings!

Usually, Marie Josèphe is modest and quiet when she speaks to my parents. It's a bit strange that she doesn't look at me and chatter away first; today, she looks at my parents first.

She's sobbing and wiping her eyes. And then she stumbles on the doorstep and falls into the room. Her black hair falls out of her cap and hangs over one eye. Tears streak her ruddy, round face. Then she looks at us. "The English officer has been here?" she asks. "Yes," she answers herself, looking around at us: so quiet with no children laughing or dogs barking. "They must have gone to all thirty houses here in Belle Isle."

I go and hug her, my body still trembling from the shock of the soldiers' words.

"We're still trying to live with this horrible news." A wave of fear surges through me, thinking of what will happen to us and all Acadians.

"And you, Marie Josèphe?" Papa says gently, "they've been at your house? Your parents..." he stops, looking for a kind word.

Marie Josèphe's voice rises, "Yes, those foul men broke into our kitchen. And my parents don't understand. They are so old," Marie Josèphe shakes her head, "Very bad with us."

She stumbles as she walks towards the three of us at the table. Maman reaches for her arm to steady her, says "Sit," and leads her to our one chair.

Marie Josèphe sits, she looks down, then up, her mouth half-open, tears running down her cheeks. "The English, why would they suddenly do this?" she asks, and the words rush out of her mouth like pounding rain.

"Daughter," Papa says. He uses the word that shows how we always think of her; as part of our family and perhaps wife to my brother, Pierre. "I think that for years, they've hoped to get our lands and our cattle."

"What happened when the English came to your house?" I ask quietly.

She buries her face in her hands and then looks up. "After the soldier left, Papa sat with his arms around Maman. They could not speak."

Marie Josèphe looks at Maman. "You know how old they are. Next summer, they were preparing to go and live with my married sister, Anna-Marie, in Grand Pre. But now my sister and her family are gone, removed by that evil man, Colonel Winslow, and put on the ships. I heard word of this but did not want to tell them, hoping I could find another place for them to live in their last years."

Marie Josèphe sighs, wearily. "So after the English soldier left, my parents sat like stones. I tried to console them but Papa suddenly jerked away and left. Maman and I clung to each other and then shakily got up to think what we should take on the ships. The cow was mooing and when I went out to the barn, and went up to fork her some hay, I found Papa." Marie Josèphe stops and weeps.

The door opens quietly. It's my brother, Pierre.

Pierre's face brightens as he sees Marie Josèphe. He puts his arm around her shoulder. "What about your Papa," he asks gently.

hayloft. At his side was a gun that he had hidden in the hay and brought out. I think he was planning to use it on himself." She wipes her eyes, and her voice drops to a whisper. "Later Papa and Maman told me that they would just as soon die here in the land where they have buried four children, as to be hauled away on a ship."

"I will go to your house, child," Papa says. "I will talk to them and pray with them. God grant them peace of heart in these terrible times."

"If my parents agree, may we travel by sea with you?" Marie Josèphe asks. She does not dare to turn and look at Pierre.

"Certainly, my child," Papa answers.

I see Pierre's face: love and anger sweep across it. I don't know if he can even speak.

"Try to give your parents hope," Pierre finally says. He holds Marie Josèphe in his arms and kisses her. Marie Josèphe stands, alone, for a moment, then turns to leave.

"I'll ask another man to help her Papa, lest he gives up completely," Papa says as he wraps seal skins around his shoulders to go out in the cold.

"Those beasts," Pierre spits out as he follows Papa out the door.

The little children look at me, their faces lined with worry. But Maman is crying, and I look to help her first.

CHAPTER SIX

MAMAN

Soon the table is covered with food, pots, dishes and baskets, little bits of our... life. Then Maman, strange for her, suddenly sits quietly on a bench. Light falls across her shoulder and onto our long table. Maman seems in a trance and picks things up, one after another, runs her fingers over them, brings them close to her eyes, looks at them again and puts them down. She picks up our large pottery pitcher with the green glaze and runs her fingers over the rough base. She puts it down.

Maman is muttering prayers in French. Her hair is messy, and a smudge of ash is on her cheek. She does not seem to know that anyone else is in the room with her. Her legs are covered in the old coverlet that her mother gave her. Running her hand over the faded squares, she picks at dangling threads with her fingers, she picks the quilt up and kisses it. Then as we watch, she gets up from the bench, gathers the quilt and throws it into the hearth-fire.

Not wanting to wake her from what seems to be a spell, we see as Maman pokes the smoldering quilt with a fire iron and shifts a slow-burning log right on top of it. "It is gone," she says, "the old life. We cannot live in that time anymore."

"Maman?" I say. "I brought the milk. Shall we leave it to settle for butter or do you want us to use it now?"

Maman seems to come back into her daily mind and looks at us. "Rose," she says. But she cannot go on. "Rose, the two little ones need milk," she finally says, "put it in a bowl on the table."

My eyes fill with tears as I look at her. Maman is not Maman. The shock of this news has shattered her. Both my parents are now more like children. It is Pierre and I who must take charge. Pierre is more ready than I. He is a man in the making. But I have to do as well as I can.

"It is as the officer says," Papa declares. "Major Handfield has tried in the last weeks to fight off this action. But he can do little now. His own wife may be sent away."

"But we can still escape," Papa announces in the commanding voice he had a few years ago. "With help from the Mi'kmaq, we can hide in the forests, or we can find others to sail across la Baie de Fundy to St. John's River colony. There the English will not capture us."

Maman looks sideways at him, "Charles, Charles. That we might have done that a few years ago when you were young and strong. But now, even my knee fails if I walk far, and your... pain in your chest and short breath... it's all too much for us now."

"I wonder," Maman asks, who seems to have come back to her usual self, "If Handfield will just let the young and strong disappear into the forests, that is the least he could do. But for us families, it will be the ships, the ships, God help us all."

Papa, Pierre, and I talk quietly in the corner and as we turn to our room, the smell of ham fills my nose. I realize that ham bakes in the oven. Pots of butter, crocks of blackberry jam, apple tarts, chunks of salt pork and cheese, heads of cabbage, bowls of eggs, turnips, dried fish: they all litter the table.

So much food! It looks as though that in her deep sorrow, Maman has gone down to the cellar for eggs and up to the attic for hams. She cooks apples and turnips in overflowing pots. Does she think that we need to eat to be strong, to face what lies ahead? Or is her mind overcome and she has lost her senses. I have never, even on Feast Days, seen such a plentiful feast. And most of it, I fear, will be left behind us on this table.

As Maman says, we cannot run to the forest and seek help from the Mi'kmaq, we cannot make our way to la Baie de Fundy and try to escape to St John's River. We are trapped here in Belle Isle to face whatever happens. Why? Mostly, because of Papa. It is sick Papa who holds us here. He is not strong enough to move fast or survive months in the woods, even though he may think he is strong and canny enough to outfox the English.

"Papa, you know we cannot take long treks through the woods now, in the dead of winter." The words burst out of my mouth.

I put up my hand to my mouth, but the words have been said. Maman looks at me, that is all she needs to do. To speak strongly can help, but it can also hurt.

Papa's eyes water as he gazes at me, and my heart sinks. He looks so much weaker than he did even a few days ago. His beard is sunken into his face, as are his eyes. He has not eaten well since he fell in the pasture with a pain so strong, he said, that it felt like his chest was cruched by a falling boulder.

Now Papa's gentle eyes rest upon me. He will not reprove me for my outburst as he does, sometimes. He does not hold himself as always right.

A branch crackles in the fire. We look nervously at each other...

"Yet, all may be well," Maman says, and sighs deeply.

I bring a warm shawl to her. "Come sit with me for a moment, Maman." I wrap her shoulders and feel the frailness of her bones through the wool. "We all must stay strong, through this hard time."

It is good for her to eat, I think. We both sit and nibble on the feast food on the table.

"Rose," Maman says, "I'm going down the path to talk to Annette and Roy. Roy's Papa trades in Boston. I'll see if they have a plan to escape. But," she rubs her arm across her forehead, "What can we do? It's too late for us to tramp across the forests."

I think of my Mi'kmaq friend, Running Deer, who lives in the forest. The last time we were together, we searched for reeds near the river. Her quick fingers finished a basket long before mine did. But Running Deer has left now. The Mi'kmaq may not return here, now. The natives probably are settled in their winter villages very deep in the forest.

These extra English soldiers brought up here from Boston by Governor Shirley of Massachusetts are too many and too well-armed for the Mi'kmaqs to attack.

Gradually, it comes to me. I may never see my friend Running Deer again.

"Wipe your tears, Rose," Maman says softly. "I will go now. You all must eat and wrap food for travel and, you must help your brothers and sister get ready."

She looks at Madeleine, "Do you still have Marie's dolly?" Madeleine runs to her bed and pulls out a rag doll. "*Bien*," Maman says smiling, "I'll bring it with me when I visit Annette and Roy, to return to Marie."

Maman wraps a cloak over her shawl, goes to the heavy door, opens it into blowing snow, and steps outside.

Madeleine and Jacques, their eyes big with fright, are watching me. They hold hands.

I get up from the bench where Papa sits still staring at the fire. I hold out my arms to the little ones and they dash into them. They are sobbing and I try to hold them so that they can feel my arms securely around them. I bend over them and rest my chin on Jacques' spiky black hair. "So, so," I croon, "Papa is here, I am here, we will take care of you."

Jacques looks up and says, "And I'll take care of sister, Maddy." He plants a sloppy kiss on her tangled black hair.

"I know you will, Jacques," I try to smile, "and when your big brother, Pierre, comes home, you can help him protect us all." Jacques shakes his head up and down, "yes."

Gently, I set the little ones on their feet and say, "Now though, Jacques and Madeleine must help sister Rose get ready for an adventure on a big ship."

"Will we sail away, out of Bay Fundy?" Jacques's voice nearly cracks with excitement. "Will we be able to catch fish? Big fish like Oncle Etienne catches in his fishing boat?"

I hug my little brother whose dark eyes sparkle at the thought of an adventure on the sea. "We may not catch fish, little brother, but who knows what we will see. You must take a little sac with your Mi'kmaq moccasins and the fishhooks that your big brother, Pierre, whittled for you, your clothes and some of your other treasures."

I quickly wipe a tear from the corner of my eye so that the little boy does not see it. "And you must bring your little whistle to keep our hearts merry with your tunes."

"*Oui*, sister Rose," Jacques skips away to gather his things.

I turn to Madeleine who is clutching her tattered baby blanket and sucking her thumb. "Now," I say briskly to her, "you must bring Foufou, your dollie, for the trip, eh?"

Madeleine takes her thumb out of her mouth and runs to our bed-in-the-wall. She grabs the floppy stuffed bird, dances back and shows it proudly to me.

"Good, good," I say quietly to her. "Now, you and Foufou snuggle into bed," I give Madeleine a tiny shove, and she skips across the floor to our shared bed-in-the-wall. It's built out of the room's wall like a big cupboard with a space in the front for us to get into it and blankets and pillows piled up inside to keep us warm on frigid winter nights.

Then I go to sit beside Papa just as the door creaks and opens and Maman walks in, the shoulders of her cloak covered with snowflakes. Papa looks up. I feel his body trembling as he asks, "What did you learn, Cécile?"

Maman carefully hangs her cloak on a hook near the door before she turns towards us. "*Rien*. Nothing," she says. She stamps her snow-covered wooden shoes. "English soldiers are everywhere. No one will say a word of their plans that might be heard by the soldiers."

We sit silently. Maman goes to the stove and hoists a big black pot of *soupe aux pois*, leftover from last midday, onto a hook and swings it over the embers. She puts bread to rest in front of the hearth. After throwing kindling branches on top of the embers, she stands up, still bent over as if in pain and then turns towards Papa. "Charles, can you put a log in there?"

She steps aside to let him do that and then, stirring the soup with a long spoon, she mutters, "How can the English do this! Horrible, *horrible*! They treat us like animals... Charles, are you all right?" She sits now beside

Papa, who holds a hand to his chest. She takes his other hand. "Is it that pain in your chest?"

Papa shakes his head, "*Non*, Cécile, not now. Before…" he looks at her and shakes his head. Maman throws her arms around his neck, then they sit back and stare into the flickering flames as the fire catches.

I speak out, cannot stop, "They are beasts, beasts! The smug smile on that officer's face! He cares nothing for what he does… if I had a gun, I would shoot him dead!"

"Rose, stop!" Maman says quietly. The held anger in her voice hits me like a blow.

With deep breaths, I calm myself. But I don't lose my rising anger. Still, whatever…and the thought scares me so much…is ahead, I want to help Maman and Papa.

Jacques quietly comes and stands by me. He seems, sometimes, much older than his six years.

Maman speaks to me again, "Rose, you're fourteen now. You know that for many of your years, you've heard us talk about the English, how they want all Acadians to pledge loyalty to England and fight with them if they fight against France?"

"Yes. But I never listened much."

Papa moves, puts his elbows on the table between us, and looks directly at me, with his eyes clear and his voice bold as it used to be. "With all the battles back and forth, we Acadians have strong roots here, stronger than the English."

Papa adds, "But, finally after wars between the English and the French, the English have gained absolute control here, especially after the Treaty of Utrecht which ended those wars and awarded Acadia to England."

"Still… we Acadians have been so successful as farmers and raising farm animals and fine horses and," he smiles at Maman, "our families have grown so much that perhaps the English envy us, and fear us as well."

"Yes, but, I still don't see why this all is happening to us now!" I burst out.

Papa says quietly, "Rose, I don't either. But friends told me a few days ago, that the English, who won a battle at Fort Beauséjour, found some of our Acadian men inside, fighting for the French. We had promised to be neutral. If Governor Lawrence heard this… he has no love for us, Acadians… maybe he decided to punish us, "Papa shakes his head, "perhaps the Governor just wants to be rid of us."

Thump! Our door shakes but does not break. We all jump up. But no one rattles the latch. It might have been a blowing branch.

CHAPTER SEVEN

FAREWELL

I stir up the fire embers to flame. For a few precious moments, I sit down to soak in the sights, the smells, the memories of my home. The fire crackles and snaps with a new log Papa added. All over the table are pieces of my life and food from our prosperous farm: salt pork, our apples, potatoes, carrots, turnips, hunks of frozen beef from our cellar, loaves of bread made with wheat from our tidal fields, green pottery from Saintonge that Jean's Papa got in a trade for his apples, from Boston.

But these are just things, things, my old dog whimpers as in his sleep as he lies at my feet. I can hear the chickens, cackling as they move about in their winter coop underneath us. And PLUME, Plume... my eyes tear, we must leave him behind. I must... Maman... *Oh mon Dieu, c'est fini. Mon Dieu.*

And then I hear again, a sharp rap, rap, on the door.

Whatever or whoever it is, I must help Papa. I go to open the door. Outside, is a young English soldier; his eyes downcast, as if he does not want to say what he has been ordered to say. Several officers on horses wait on the roadway.

"*C'est l'heure!*" he says.

Papa's hand is on my shoulder. He takes it away and stands straight. "How can you do this?" he says, his voice trembling with anger.

"Gov'nor Lawrence's orders," the young man answers with a toss of his head.

The frantic moos of cows fill our ears. The English are driving all the village cattle away.

The young soldier says again. "You must leave today to the harbor. The ships are waiting." Another older, larger soldier stamps up beside him and bellows, "Get ready. Out! Everyone! Out!"

Papa rushes out of the house. He raises his arms above his head and shouts, "We're going to Sainte Jean Baptiste Church. Today's Our Lady's Feast Day. Good Queen Anne gave us the right."

"You are not!"

Papa is hit hard on the back with the musket of an English soldier. His legs give way, and he falls to the cold, snowy ground.

"Get ready to board the ships! *Vite!*" the man orders again.

"You Beast! How can you hit my Papa like that! You are savages!" I scream.

I rush to help Papa up. The officer stares at Papa. "*Monsieur*, now is the time," he says flatly. "It is a sad time. But the time has come. You and your family should move with all haste with your belongings in one cart, to board the ships."

Papa cannot speak. He turns back to the house, his shoulders slumped, and his gait unsteady. I walk with him. My poor, dear Papa. He is crying. I grab his hand.

The hubbub of crying children, creaking wagons being loaded, frantic screaming mothers, fills our ears.

Our door swings open back into the house. Maman rushes about with baskets of food. I think to gather more eggs from the chickens in the barn. We set Madeleine to wrapping cheeses in linen. Our tears stream as we work in our house for the last time. Where are we going? We have no idea.

Freezing air from outside swirls about the room through the door Maman has left open. Shivering, I poke the fire embers, reach into the woodpile near the hearth, and throw small and big logs into the fire in an effort to warm the frigid December air. Finally, Papa staggers over to the door and bangs it closed.

The little ones come to the table and snatch goodies of all kinds and stomachs filled, they go back to their beds and begin to pull out more of their favorite toys, balls, fishing rods, shells, and favorite bird feathers. I throw Jacques a leather sac and tell him, "Only what will fit in this."

Papa tells me to gather all our bed coverings and he loads them into our big trunk. How we can carry it to the wagon, I don't know, with Pierre gone.

I try to gather my treasures; a little pottery dove, *Espère*, that André gave me, a tiny crucifix, combs and pins and fancy scarves and put them into one small leather sack and finally take it to the trunk. I put my special fricot pan in another leather sac ready to carry with me. If only Pierre were here to help with the heavy things, I think, when a young friend of his, Jean, walks in the door.

Jean's the son of our closest neighbor. His father, having done well with sales of grain from the dyked lands, has taken him to far-off places like Louisbourg and the West Indies to trade furs, grain, and cattle from his tidal fields. Jean knows the world.

"Pierre sent me," he says, "Pierre and others are trying to delay the English officers from giving the final order to leave." He puts a hand on my shoulder and nods.

"Can you get the ox hitched up to the cart, Jean?... It would help so much."

He turns, and the little ones clamor to go with him and I let them, their last visit to Plume our lovely horse and Brun our ox. But they do not know this yet.

I drop my head and cannot stop crying, I love those animals, Plume has taken me on trips up into the forest, on wild gallops, and into Annapolis Royal. He is my best friend that I can tell things to and he'll never tell. To think I'll never feel his warm breath on my hands, hear his nicker as I come to his stall. What will they do with him... Oh, this is sad, sad. I sob.

They are coming back; I can hear Jacques excited chatter with Jean. I must, just go on.

Papa goes outside to relieve himself and while he is gone, I poke around in the drawer underneath their bed-in-the-wall for Papa's extra pair of breeches and his feast day vest along with a fur hat like a hood. Maman has started a trunk with her things and adds Papa's clothes to that. On top of the trunk, she throws a bear skin to keep her and Papa warm on the ship.

Now we begin to hear soldiers outside urging everyone on with shouts and musket shots in the air. We miss Pierre. Jean helps with the heaviest things, trying to pack the cart. But we have far too much for one cart.

"Maman," I say loudly, as I am tired and angry at what has happened. "So, we'll take two carts."

"One cart, they said, Rose," Maman mutters.

"*NON*" I say a little louder than I wish. "We can use the little cart for treats for Papa: dried apples, cranberries, salmon and moose strips, dried cod, bread and apple tarts and we can put in extra furs to use and trade as well…" I say. "They'll not notice."

Maman's eyes brighten. "That's a good idea, Rose. And those foods will tempt him to eat."

"We have a lot of salt pork, so we can put some in both carts. And I have one pottery jar with a thick cover; we'll put the spruce beer in the small cart for Papa. And we can add our chaudron pot that Jean's father got for us from Boston and maybe on top the two short benches Papa made."

Jean runs to the barn and brings back our everyday cart hitched to our young ox. We pile Papa's food and the other household things into the little cart, but my head is as jumbled as all our possessions lying around our house. How can we ever survive this journey to an unknown, will we be together on the ship, where is Pierre?

Poor little Madeleine is in her bed in the wall, weeping so loudly that I can hear her. I have to go and drag her out.

Now she's screaming and holding onto the wall of her bed. Jacques finally goes to her and holds out his hand for her to hold onto and moves from the nest of her bed. Maman sees her and comes and scoops her up saying, "Come, Maddy, you can travel with Maman in our own little cart." And Madeleine goes along and stops screaming.

Jacques and Jean quickly pack Pierre's things and put them into the big wagon and then Jean, turns to Maman and tells her he must leave, that their family will try to stay close to us on the way to the ships.

English soldiers rush everywhere, yelling and threatening. Finally, we have stuffed as much as we can into the two carts. Papa stands by the big cart fiddling with the leather straps that hold the ox to the cart. Jacques sits on the floor holding our dog and weeping.

"*Allons*," Maman finally says, wiping tears from her face. "We must start, or the soldiers will come back and hurt us.". We kneel together, and Papa prays for our friends. We leave weeping, the home of our hearts.

Maman drives the little cart with Madeline beside her onto the road towards the harbor at Annapolis Royal. The road is rutted with slabs of ice, filled with lumbering carts. English soldiers yell at the teams. Several families from Belle Isle are directed onto the road in front of us. Finally, the English soldiers wave at us to join the sad column of forsaken people.

Papa climbs up into the big ox cart so slowly that Maman, with Madeleine beside her, is away before we start. I sit beside Papa. Jacques perches on the hay behind us, interested and waving at his friends. And then I smell smoke. A black cloud drifts around the river. Someone calls desperately, "They are burning my house!" I look back and, sadly, see it.

Behind us on the road, I see my best friend, Marie Josèphe. She drives their cart pulled by one ancient bullock. Beside her hunches her Papa. Her old Maman, wrapped in furs in the back of the cart, waves gaily waves as if she has lost her mind from the shock of all this.

Soldiers crack whips at young children walking because their families are so large, they cannot fit in their wagon. The children scream back at them and beyond control of their parents, throw rocks at the soldiers.

As we get closer to the village, Annapolis Royal, a salty wind brushes my face, and the crashing sound of the huge tides of la Baie de Fundy fills my ears.

On the beach across from Goat Island, an English officer stands high on a platform; directing wagons and ordering people to board longboats to take them out to the maybe six or seven brigantines in the wide river near Goat Island. We can just see the big ships, with their big square sails moving about. They look like the cargo ships that Jean's Papa and others have used to ships horses and other animals to the West Indies. Papa calls them brigs.

A bullock cart with no driver crashes into empty carts tipped onto the sand. Trunks and quilts and baskets lie spread open and abandoned.

An English officer standing on a bench near the water sees Maman's little wagon ahead of us and points to a space on the beach far away from us. I scream desperately to Maman and she turns, realizes how far behind we are and tries to stop. But a lone soldier grabs her ox harness and drags him where the officer points. The officer continues to direct his troops with cool precision to load the ship. We are getting farther and farther from her.

Papa does not notice where Maman is headed. He tries to control our ox which is trotting away from Maman in the confusion of wagons and people. Our wagon now is squeezed to the right of the beach by the press of wagons behind us. From the back of the wagon with Jacques, I scream at Papa to steer towards Maman's cart and then hang onto Jacques, lest he falls off and is trampled.

Then I see Maman at a far away stretch of beach, steering her little cart near to André's maman. I jump down and try to turn our ox cart in her direction. I call, "That way!" pointing down the beach towards Maman but Papa is deaf with the noise and confusion and does not turn the ox.

In the next few minutes, Maman and Madeleine, along with André and his maman are rudely forced out of their carts onto the beach. Soldiers gather all their bundles and throw them into a longboat, Maman clutches Madeleine and looks about frantically.

Screaming, I grab Papa's arm again, and point towards them. I jump from our cart and run after Maman, but I am too late. She and Madeleine are now in a boat…

Papa's eyes, filled with blowing sand, probably cannot see Maman.She, with Madeleine, André, and his mother sit in a boat heading towards a square sailed ship. Soldiers stop me and Jacques from moving from our sea-weed-strewn section of the beach towards where Maman left the beach.

I can just barely hear Maman's screams," Rose! Charles! Jacques!" as I stumble back to find Papa in the melee of carts, people and soldiers scattered about me. All around us, people load into ship's boats. Many families of our village. Wails of anguish fill my ears. My eyes fill with tears. I can no longer see Maman and Madeleine.

One of Major Handfield's men sees us. "Over there! Take them to THE EXPERIMENT," the officer calls. And then, a bearded old English soldier grabs me by the arm. "Your turn," he says in French. "Which are your things?" he asks. He points them out to the soldier beside him. The man loads some of our bundles into a boat pulled partially out of the water onto the sand.

As he turns towards the waiting long boat, he sees Papa. "Your father?" he asks. I nod and try to break away from the soldier to get Papa and help him stand up. The man lets me go and I stand beside Papa, and take his gnarled hand and gently pull him erect. His eyes watering from the cold, he stands up shakily. I pull gently at his hand, but he stands still and cannot move his feet out of the wet sand into which they have sunk. The officer waves to two younger men and they form a chair out of their hands and carry him into the boat, leaving Jacques and me on the beach with men guarding us.

I scream frantically, "He's my Papa. Let us go with him," trying to break away from the soldier who holds me. The officer seeing this, waves me and Jacques towards the water where we must step into the freezing shallows, walk to the boat, and get pulled in.

The sailors wait to take oars and when they do, they row our boat with slow jerks out into the deep water. There are about twenty people and our assorted belongings in the boat. I squat near Papa and rub his hands and his back and tell him we are with him. But he hardly opens his eyes, he is like a living haunt, my dear Papa… my heart feels so badly seeing him like this. Jacques begins to weep calling in gulps, "Papa, Papa," but Papa hardly opens his eyes. We cover him as we can from the splashing water.

Around us are about ten longboats like ours stuffed with people, trunks, sacs, and odd chairs and small benches. I hear the officer behind me scream out a command, "to The Experiment," and point.

Then, I see it, the ship we are to board, THE EXPERIMENT, a large two-masted, square sailed ship surrounded by small boats like ours. Then I see, too, Pierre and Marie Josèphe not far from us, in a longboat heading towards The Experiment. How did he get here? I pray they load him on our ship.

Above, suddenly, I hear Madeleine's scream and Maman's wail of anguish. Directly over our head is the deck of THE SNOW. Maman is at the ship's railing. She holds my sister in one arm and tries to plunge off the deck into our boat or the frigid water.

I see André's mother beside Maman, trying to hold her back. But why is André's mother still in Acadia? She and André were to leave Acadia earlier... André holds Maman and pulls her back from the edge of the deck. Then I hear only Maman's screams.

CHAPTER EIGHT

THE SHIP

With a violent thump, our longboat crashes into The Experiment. Sitting on a middle plank as I am, my body jolts forward into the woman in front of me, and she nearly goes over the side. I grab her shoulder, and she lands back on the bench.

Around us in the harbor, I see people from longboats climbing up swinging rope ladders to reach the ships' decks. I watch them, as I cling to the sides of our longboat. How can I ever do that? The crewman in the front of our boat looks at Papa, waves his arm for him to go up and yells over the wind, "Make haste."

Waves are battering our boat, sloshing water over the sides. A young sailor bails constantly. I try to help Papa grab the ends of the ladder. But he cannot stand up. A sailor bellows up to the deck and a rope chair drops. Papa is bundled in, with Jacques on his lap. I kiss them both and they are lifted upward.

I try to cling to the cold, wet, ladder flopping in and out of the boat when another longboat hits ours, and I fall back. I get up and Pierre is in the other boat, his face bloodied and one eye swollen. He snatches at a ladder and climbs upward easily; he's used to fishing boats and loading onto larger ships. He has put Marie Josèphe in front of him, holding her body into the ship with his.

Seeing them gives me courage. I grab the ladder again and try, and finally get up to the deck. Papa slumps in a heap at the foot of a mast. Pierre, Marie Josèphe and Jacques stand with him and after I catch my breath, I crawl over to them and stand with them, looking sadly at Papa. Pierre squats down beside him, "Papa, we are here. We are on the ship now."

Papa opens his eyes and sees us all. He holds his arms out as if he were to grasp us all in a big wide armed hug. Then he closes his eyes and says softly, "God bless us all," and his head drops, and he is asleep or unaware. I go and hug Pierre and Marie Josèphe. "Thank God, you are here." We sit around Papa and look at the people on deck with us. Only a few are from Belle Isle.

Snatching us all from the beach in a random way, the English have broken up villages, and families, as we have lost ours.

Cold December air steals through my fine wet woolen striped skirt, as I stand at the ship's rail, looking back at our dear land. My face crinkles as a dry leaf does, as tears stream over my cheeks. All around us, big ships are raising their sails to catch the stiff breezes off la Baie de Fundy. I look back at my dear land, its rivers and mountains and marshes, and I despair, I will never see it again.

The Experiment sails past Maman's ship, the wind quickens, and we glide into la Baie de Fundy. We've been told that we will be on this ship about twenty-eight days. Can all of us live that long? How will be able to breathe, packed into the bottom of the ship, with hundreds of other people? The sailors raise more sails as we reach the open waters of the ocean. I hear the sail canvas cracking in the wind and look up, to see the sails billowing over me, when I feel a little hand in my hand.

"Jacques! Are you all right?"

"*Mais Oui*! The sailors let me coil some ropes for them, and they tell me I'll be a fine sailor." His black hair blows in the wind, his cheeks redden as he looks up at me with a big smile, missing his two front teeth. To Jacques, all life is a great adventure.

And Maman, how will she survive, with no Papa or Pierre to help her fight for food and air. Oh my God, you have forgotten us. I bow my head and pray and then a sailor grabs my arm and pushes me toward the opening of the hold. He shoves me hard, and I stumble and fall.

When I wake up, I am stretched out flat on the rough wood floor in the hold of the ship. My knee throbs with pain. My eyes slowly focus on Marie Josèphe and Pierre who bend over me. Marie Josèphe holds a tin cup of water in her hand and brings it to my lips.

I gulp the water. Pierre puts his arm behind my back and helps me sit up. His eye is swollen shut, but he manages a crooked grin.

"Rose, anything broken?"

"My knee hurts. But I don't think so."

"Rose, we need to work together now."

"*Oui*, Pierre."

We've had our struggles between us, Pierre and I. He's three years older and likes to order me around. But we're not in our farmyard anymore. We're on a desperate journey. I grip one of his hands and his strong, warm grip gives me hope. Then I look around.

At the far end of the hold, live bodies lies stretched out flat on the floor, tightly packed, shoulder to shoulder.

I turn to Marie Josèphe, "Do you know why they're lying down like that?"

She shrugs, "Maybe they're sick, or want to stretch out. No one can stand straight here except the children."

Pierre says, "One sailor on the deck, he's from Acadia and forced to sail, told me to be prepared. '*C'est terrible*,' he said. "The ships' hold, where they carry cargo, that's what they call these big spaces, 'holds" was re-made into three holds, one on top of the other. The height of each hold is a little over four feet."

Marie Josèphe screws up her face, chews on her pipe stem and takes it out, ready to spit and instead says, "We're pigs in a pen, with no pots or places for us to relieve ourselves!"

Pierre butts in, "They say they'll let six of us out together every once in a while, to get air."

"How will we survive?" Marie Josèphe near screams.

Pierre shakes his head, "Only if we don't get sick."

I can now see that only children like Jacques can stand up straight. The space we are in is no higher than the height of a big barrel.

Pierre waits until I have settled myself and says, "We have to sleep in shifts. There's not enough room for us all to lie down at the same time."

After these words sink into my brain, I remember. "Papa, where is Papa?" I cry.

"He is below," Marie Josèphe says, "The weak people have been put into the bottom bilge hold of the ship, for fear they have small-pox."

"But he's not sick with a disease. He has a weak heart."

Marie Josèphe scowls, "The English don't care enough to find that out. 'We need to make room for the healthy,'" a French-speaking sailor told me.

"Pierre, can we go to Papa?" My voice trembles. Pierre turns away from me and rubs his eyes.

"Tonight, Rose," Pierre says. "After the sailors close the top hatch for the night: The trap door to the bottom hold is blocked with heavy planks. But I can move them."

The ship sails calmly and I fall asleep. I wake up to see that Pierre has laid the hatch door open. A few others of us who have relatives below crowd down the stairs into the depths of the ship. Dark as the depths of a deep cave, the top of the space here is lower than the upper hold. The smell of body waste and foul water chokes our throats. Frigid air bites our faces and hands. We feel our way along in darkness calling "Charles," for Papa. Several others call "Papa."

We crawl past limp bodies that barely breathe. Do we hear Papa's faint voice? We see Papa's coat. And then we see him. He lies crumpled like a sheet on the rough board floor. Under his head, he has managed to put one of our quilts. Leakage water seeps around his body when the ship changes course.

Papa sees us. He finally calls feebly. "Where is my love? Where is Cécile?"

I lie to him, thinking of Maman, who must now be weeping on a different ship, missing Papa so much that her heart is breaking. "Papa, she was forced to stay in a different part of this ship. They will not let her come to you." I can't bear to tell him the truth: that she is on another ship and we have little hope we will ever see her and our little sister, Madeleine, again.

Pierre scratches a flint and lights a precious candle stub. We see Papa's eyes flicker like fire embers. He turns away from us. I gasp as I see a shadowy shape running behind him.

Tears well up in my eyes. Pierre sits down and pulls Papa up so that he can hold him in a bear hug. He whispers, "The sailors put you here because they fear you have small-pox. We will carry you to where we are. The sailors may not even notice."

Papa's eyes wander. His eyes close and he drops his head. Pierre lifts his frail body and puts Papa on his shoulder like he is carrying a calf to a field. We stagger past bodies and up the ladder and Pierre lays Papa down in the upper hold, far away from the trap door. All is quiet and after the others who went down to see family members, get out, Pierre quickly replaces the planks across the trap door.

Marie Josèphe comes and sits beside us. "How is he?" she asks.

Pierre shakes his head. "He's very bad. He doesn't have small-pox but he's very weak."

"I think I saw a rat down there. He may have been bitten," I say. "It was terrible." We three huddle around Papa, until his shoulders barely rise and fall, and he sleeps.

Pierre holds out his hands and Marie Josèphe and I each take one. "We'll do our best to help Papa," he says. "But who can fix a broken heart?"

"Couldn't we all rise against these foul English sailors?" Marie Josèphe asks.

"Without guns, swords or even sticks, and with us put in different holding pens," Pierre shakes his head. "NO. Let's try to rest and see what we can do for Papa."

I lean back against the ship's side and try to rest.

Deep sobs rise in my throat, and I can hardly breathe. Closing my eyes, I pray for us all. I must do everything I can to help Papa. This is why I didn't go with André. My fate is to help our family survive. I lost Maman, I must help Papa.

Pictures slip into my heart. I remember how Papa held me on his lap as Maman spun out her tales and when he snatched me out of the big boar's pen when the boar had knocked me down. One day Papa came home with a bulging sack and in it was my dear dog, Gardien. But the day I remember best was when Papa threw me up on our fine horse Plume and first helped me ride him in the pasture... Papa... Papa, I cover my face with my hands and weep.

"What can we do?" Marie Josèphe whispers, "he's so frail."

"He needs food," I say. "Good food. I doubt he can chew much. Who knows what they will feed him or us. If only we had all the food we packed. But it's all with Maman or on the beach." I shake my head and cover my eyes and try to think. When we were let out for air, I saw a cow in a pen on the deck.

"There's a cow on board that's giving the sailors trouble. I'll offer to milk her in exchange for a cup of milk each for Papa and Jacques."

Early on the fourth day out from Annapolis Royal, when the captain stops to yell at a young sailor in the cow's pen on the deck, for not keeping the cow clean and milking her calmly, I fall to my knees in front of him.

I make hand signals of milking. The Captain's ruddy bewhiskered face looks down at me. I can tell that he does not understand much of what I say. I point at the cow and again make milking motions with my hands.

A rough, grimy hand dangles in front of my eyes, "Up!" the captain says, points to the cow, and nods. The captain looks at me, I feel his eyes hungrily gazing at me. It is as though he sees me now as a girl, not as an animal to be shipped to a new port.

The captain walks toward the entryway of his cabin on the rear deck, then glances back, "Come!" he commands, "Get bucket." I standstill. I'll be all alone down there.

Jean, our friend from Annapolis-Royal, makes a sound. Jean's dark eyes lock with mine, and I see caution in them.

But just now I am willing to do anything to win the captain's favor, to save my father's life. So I boldly speak, "*Mais Oui*," although the words are loud, they are false honor. I'm just speaking out to help Papa.

Scuttling over the now pitching deck like a crab, I follow the captain. Then I go down a small flight of stairs and stand crammed into a tiny space, in front of a door. I am old enough to worry about going into this place with a strange man.

The captain tramps down the stairs, crowds behind me and reaches around me to open the door. "In," he says roughly and pushes me into the space. Far from the smell of vomit and crying voices, I am in a pleasant room that stretches under the width of the deck. The captain's bunk is to the side and in the center of the room is a round shiny wood table, covered with sailing charts and surrounded by leather chairs.

Astounded by the quiet elegance of his room, I stop short.

He grabs my arm and pulls me farther into the room, "You, *vous belle*, eh?" his words and the look on his face frighten me.

I stare at him, confused by his mixed words. Then I have a sense of what might happen next.

"NO!" I scream.

Looking up desperately, I see a crucifix on the ship's wall. Besides it hangs a small painting of him with his family, his wife and two young girls, his daughters. I point at the painting of the girls and the crucifix and shake my head violently. "No! *Non!*" I point at the painting again. "Rose, good girl."

He looks ashamed, the captain does. Sinking onto the bed himself, he says, "*C'est un terrible voyage. Terrible!*" He looks at me with some kindness.

Perhaps he has a heart under his uniform, I think. Still not hoping for much, I stammer slowly and make milking motions with my fingers, and then cup my hand as if I was holding a cup, throw my head back as if I am swallowing the milk, then hold up two fingers and mimic a cup.

The captain nods, hands me a clean bucket and two cups, and points toward the cabin door.

I gasp and run up the short stairs to the deck. Pierre and Jean stand waiting anxiously.

"I'm all right," I say.

On deck, I'm near frozen. The freezing winter wind whips my long skirt. I clutch the bucket. A sailor is standing in the middle of a group of Acadians on deck. "Food," he calls loudly. I lurch over, remembering the feast of ham and turnips and sweets we had the night before we left.

I know this is my only chance for food for the day. I grab a hunk of moldy bread and a hunk of dried meat. I force myself not to look, just put it in my mouth and chew. I sense the maggots in the meat. The food comes up and I have to run to the deck rail. I'm weaker than when we got on this ship. Several hunks of bread and a lump of salt pork are food for swine, and that's all I have to eat each day.

Then, I go to milk. I slide close to the cow's pen to stroke her curly hair between her eyes, to stroke her flank, to help her be calm. Then, I begin to milk. When the pail is full, the captain's aide comes to take the pail. I stop him and pull out two pottery cups from my apron, one for milk for Jacques and one for Papa.

I scoop milk into the cups. Jacques runs up freely. The sailors have taken a liking to him, with his beady sparkling eyes and his little whistle. Jacques gulps his bit of milk and runs off again.

I take a tiny sip of the other cup of milk and head for the hatch to go down into the ship. The sea is calm. I hold the cup firmly and somehow get down the stairs to the hold. Pierre, Marie Josèphe and Jean surround me to protect me and help me stay steady.

"Papa is awake," Pierre says.

I clutch the cup tightly.

"Papa smiled today," he says. Pierre points to a dark corner of the hold.

"Papa is resting over there waiting for you."

I pick my way over prone bodies and try not to gag from the stench of body waste. Then I see Papa. He has turned toward the outer wall of the ship. Does he look a little sturdier? Perhaps, or perhaps it is the coat that Pierre lent him.

I squat down and gently rub his shoulder. It feels stiff and I rub some more. And then I gently pull on his shoulder. His body falls towards me. Spit drools from his mouth.

"Pierre!" I scream. "Help Papa!"

Pierre comes quickly. He, too, puts a hand under Papa's shoulder and struggles to raise him.

Like a rag doll, his body falls forward.

"He is gone. Everything is gone!"

CHAPTER NINE

PAPA

Pierre crouches beside me, pulls me away. "Rose," he whispers, "Papa is gone. Let him go. He is out of this Hell and with the Lord." Pierre sits with me, his arm over my shoulders. "Rose, Rose," he is sobbing, "he was so weak, and you tried to give him milk. You helped him as much as you could." He helps me sit up. "I will take Marie Josèphe to help me speak to the captain. We must have prayers…" his voice trails off.

And I know then he will be buried at sea. No plot to go to, to pray, no trace left. Tears flood my face; no words are left.

In the lantern light, swaying with the ship's movement, I look at Papa's face again and know that it looks peaceful.

I throw myself into the kind woman's arms. Others come and rub my back and shoulders gently. Papa is dead. Our light and leader is gone. I moan again, "Papa!" and I think of myself.

In our captivity, I have no parent. Even though I am getting older, I still depended on the thought that we have Papa here. He is gone. We are all alone in this world on the open sea.

Pierre's face is lined with dirt and tears. "Rose," he says, "he is at peace."

I hear prayers whispered. *The Lord is my shepherd...* The Lord is my Shepherd. I see a tiny lamb playing around Papa in our farmyard in Acadia. So... Papa will be in Heaven. But he will never again walk the fields of the earth.

Jacques has been found and Pierre brings him to the body. Jacques's brown eyes flood with tears and he shakes violently. Pierre sits behind him and holds him, trying to console him. They pray the Our Father together.

Marie Josèphe tells me to lie beside her and rest. Pierre finally calms Jacques so that he sleeps. The older women cluster around Papa's body. The sailor that Marie Josèphe spoke to, brought down an old piece of canvas and the women with their stiff needles, make a loose sac for the body.

Pierre and another man lift Papa's body into the sac, and our men carry Papa's body up the steps to the deck.

He is truly gone. I have been fooling myself that he would live, that wherever we are sent, our family would be together when we land. But like many of our young friends on this ship, we will come to a new land alone.

My head drops and I weep quietly, wiping my eyes and saying nothing until my voice is steady.

I lie down to rest and pull Jacques to my side.

At dusk, we are called into a circle on deck. It is calm and the ship is barely moving. The captain says a few words which I am too upset to understand.

Acadian men lay the sac containing Papa's body in the middle of our circle. Pierre stands near the body, pauses, and bows his head, then standing straight and looking at us, says the Our Father. The captain lets each of our people do the same. I shake violently when my turn comes and cannot speak. Marie Josèphe puts her hand on my arm and we walk forward. Standing there, in the bitter wind that has picked up, I begin to sing, Jacques with his every ready tin-whistle, quickly joins in... When we finish, we go back to our place in the circle.

Then we say the words of the Psalm together: "*Le seigneur est mon berger.*". The captain makes a hand signal to his sailors. They step forward, hoist the body bag to their shoulders, rest it on the rail of the ship, and let it fall into the sea. It hits the water with a splash, floats and then sinks.

I turn away. My dear Papa, he was my heart, my joy, my guiding star. Gone. Now I realize even more how sweet and good and wise he was. Gone.

But again, the captain speaks. The sailors walk back from the foredeck with a tiny canvas bundle. A child must have died. The parents and one of our old men bless the bundle, raising their hands in the sign of the cross.

At the captain's command, the sailors carry the little bundle to the ship's rail and let it go. Our ship sails on slowly. All are quiet.

Then I hear a sailor say one word, "Sharks." And a few of the crew look over the ship's railing. I hear the smack of huge fish jumping and hitting each other. I see the horrified looks of the older Acadians who hold their children tight to their skirts. And as the wind begins to blow viciously from behind us, I see bits and pieces of the canvas bundle blowing over the sea. The child is dead, I tell myself. It does not know. But I know, and it is too terrible.

Without the experience of being a mother, I had not thought of holding Jacques close to me, so that he could not see what might happen. Jacques, so often with the sailors, had gone with them to the edge of the deck. Jacques's firm little body now crashes into me. He holds me desperately around my skirts. He screams, "the bad fish!"

All of us on the deck look at each other... I am fighting to think of the dead child and my dear Papa in the fields of Heaven, gathering lambs and ewes about themselves. They are at peace, I tell myself again and again.

But life on earth is horrible. I sink to the deck and hold Jacques on my lap. Pierre comes and stands beside me. He speaks to the people from my village who say how sad they are to lose Papa. Marie Josèphe comes. She strokes my hair, sweeping it back from my forehead, murmuring words of sorrow.

My heart breaks as I think of Papa's sad death, alone, as a prisoner, on a strange ship, separated from Maman.

Ripped from our home, village and church as we are, we do not even have our close friends and relatives near us, to close us within a warm circle of friendship. We have some of them. But after Papa's death, Papa whom I leaned on so much, my sense of the support of Acadians for each other, slides away. What good does our support for each other do for us now? We are captives, part of a herd of people the English drive forward to their pastures, not ours.

Never before have I so much felt the desperate urge to, somehow, grow into the person I am, strong for myself and others. Now, Papa is gone. Perhaps the tears I shed for him water my young self, a strong, growing girl who faces an unknown future.

The wind begins to blow viciously in gusts, whipping this huge ship back and forth like a weaver's spindle. One man is blown screaming across the deck. He is saved by a sailor's gaff viciously hooked onto his cloak.

And then Pierre pulls at my arm, and I hear Marie Josèphe's voice saying urgently, "We must get below." Sailors yell, "A gale is upon us!" We rush to the hold and hear the heavy doors slammed shut above us. We fear we will not live through the storm.

CHAPTER TEN

ESCAPE?

"Lay two quilts together on the hold floor," Pierre says, "We may have to fight for the space, but we can be together and near a way to escape from this hold to the deck, if we need to..."

"But the ship may sink!" Marie Josèphe near screams from her fear. "We may all die!"

"Quiet! Get the quilts!" Pierre yells. His jaw juts forward and he sounds like an officer giving commands. After finding our storage sacs, we get the quilts and sit trembling together on them. Pierre sits now behind Marie Josèphe with his arms around her and kisses her ear. "My love, we are together. Let us pray we survive." I put my arms around Jacques, trying to keep from shaking from fear as the ship sinks and crashes into the fierce waves.

"There are many sick with the pox," Marie whispers. "But most of them lie together at the other end of the ship. Maybe, staying apart, we will escape the sickness."

Once a day, a young sailor brings hunks of moldy bread and salt pork down to us to eat. But we hardly touch it at first, until our extreme hunger makes us eat this foul food and our stomachs cramp and our heads swim with dizzy spells. We starve, we cannot get out of this stinking place that is only four feet tall. We cannot stand up, we cannot relieve ourselves except on the floor, many of us are sick and lie moaning and screaming while the wind jolts our ship harshly side to side and up and down. And the sailors hardly enter the place to bring us water.

With such fierce winds, the sailors probably do not hoist sails on the masts, only to have them ripped in shreds within hours. Without a steady wind and a well balanced shipload, The Experiment wallows around like a nut in a whirlpool.

Pierre tells us that when the ship was fitted to carry us, many of the ballast stones and weights in the very bottom of this ship must have been removed so as to pack in more people. The ship has no steady weight in its base to keep it upright.

The steady up, down, sideways jerks of the ship go on and on… with the wind and the waves for days. We are in the midst of a hurricane cluster of storms.

Still, sick, and weak as we are, we plot an escape. It does not matter if we are shot trying, this life is near death anyway.

But our English captors are cautious. All together we Acadians boarded as a group of two hundred and fifty people, the crew numbers perhaps twenty but if they come near us in our prison, they carry guns.

Pierre and Jean talk to others. They plan what they will do; grab the sailors who carry food to us and snatch their muskets from them. Then, our men will rush up to the deck all together, overcome the crew as there are so few of them, hold the captain in chains, force him to navigate and shoot any sailor who fights against us. With the sailing skill of our Acadian seamen, we will change course and head either to the French West Indies or back to the French islands, St. Pierre and Miquelon. We may die of starvation or disease, but our wish is to be free. We may die, trying…

But the hurricane still shrieks and blows like a demon about us. It does not stop. Below we are very weak, but we still find enough Acadian men to help with an escape plan. We learn that we should have gotten to our destination twenty-eight days after we left Annapolis Royal. We are well past that number and still in the middle of the ocean. The hurricane decides our progress. We probably are still far off from any land.

While Pierre, Jean and the others are planning, I sit alone and suddenly think of Maman. Where are she and Madeleine? How will she survive, with no Papa or Pierre to help her fight for food and air?

Oh my G—, you have forgotten us all! I bow my head and pray.

Jacques is nearly the only one that remains healthy and spirited. He plays his tin whistle and tries to cheer us until one day the ship feels as if it is again sailing with sails aloft. We must move against the English sailors now or we will go to an unknown fate.

Pierre's men talk and watch the hold doors above us from where the English sailors will come with our paltry food. The group in the hold readies itself to crash against them when they come with the stinking food. It is time. But where are we?

Suddenly, the ship hits something hard, we all fall over each other. Then, without us moving forward, we hear the lookout screaming "Land!"

The doors of the hold open with a crash… Guards appear, carrying guns, looking down at us. We have no chance against them.

All hope of escape vanishes like the cloud it was, as we smell the fresh air. We push over each other to scramble up to the deck as the guards allow.

"Where are we now?" An old man I hardly know sinks to his knees and cries.

CHAPTER ELEVEN

STRANGE NEW WORLD

The misty sky brightens into the morning and fresh breezes sweep through my hair. Overhead, the sails flap and the ship rocks back and forth as it is hit by cross currents and crashes into sand bars. A huge harbor filled with large and small sailing and rowed craft, opens before us.

Marie Josèphe and I hold groggily to the deck guard rail. My legs shake and my head spins. I look cross-eyed at Marie Josèphe, "The curly-haired young sailor was good to let us stay on deck."

"Yes, but he doesn't tell us much. The last time I spoke to him, I asked him where we are going, but he shook his head. Pierre stopped me from asking him again. He says that the English lie all the time, so it is not worth my time to ask."

Out in the sunlight after weeks below deck, I see what I look like. "Your clothes aren't as ragged as mine," I say,

Pointing to a large rip in my skirt and a tear in my weskit. The breeze tugs the cap on my head. I grab it, look at it, it is filthy, and I nearly throw it into the sea, but instead I smash it back on my head to help hold down my thick hair.

Watching me, Marie Josèphe's dark eyes glint with spirit, "Is this the end of this eternal voyage?" she moans. "I stink, and my hair is filled with lice and my shoes have holes for my toes. Ugh, I can't stand myself."

"Let's at least try to make ourselves look like respectable Acadian girls, Marie Josèphe. Quick, we can dash to our sacs downstairs and try to find clean things."

Marie Josèphe looks at me as if to say, how can you bother about your clothes, when our life ahead of us is unknown...

"It may help us, so we don't get treated like cattle, like we have been for weeks. Remember, we are Acadians. We are proud of ourselves and all of us."

We look at each other and dash to the hold where we have our clothes, hastily stuck in our little trunks. We sort through things and each of us finds fresh weskit and, I can hardly believe it, each one has a fresh cap and skirt and stockings. Fast as we can, not caring who sees us, we change into our new-old clothes. Jacques and Pierre are on deck so we race to join them.

"Look, everyone's out now."

By now, all our Acadians have burst out onto the deck in the sun with us. But not all our Acadians, we lost over fifty of us from smallpox on this perilous voyage. At the end of the crowd, a straggle of children, whom I know lost their parents at sea, wander onto the deck. All of them are dressed in rags and filthy. I wave at a dear little girl watched over by a lanky bodied fellow who looks to be about seventeen.

"Well, Marie Josèphe," I say quietly, pointing at the little girl, "We don't have the worst of it…look at that poor girl her brother may be snatched away by a workman, I guess, and she…she will be left all alone." My eyes, even though I try to stop them, fill with tears for the girl. "There's nothing I can do for her," I look at Marie Josèphe. "I don't know how to help myself."

Marie Josèphe's dark eyes soften, but as always, she's honest. "No use going on about that child, now. Your heart cannot help her," she says softly.

"If my Maman were here, she would try to help her; I know she would," I say firmly.

And while Marie Josèphe goes off to see what she can find out, I stand quietly on the deck and remember, that Maman and Madeleine are gone. The last time I saw them was when they screamed down at us from another ship when we all were leaving Acadia.

But might their ship have landed here, before us? Still, my heart sinks because how would we know if she did, and where might she be in this place, New York? Marie Josèphe might have enough English words to ask about her. But no one cares. None of the English care. They are glad to be rid of us.

"Not one of the crew will say much," Marie Josèphe announces. "Our captors are so mean, they just order us around and don't tell us anything,"

She grabs my hand. Her hand is rough warm and strong. Mine is cold and bony. We shake them up and down.

"We are sisters," that's what we tell them," I say.

Around us sailors scream commands at each other. And although I know little English, I think that I hear the words, "New York." And I guess that where we are. But where will we go next?

I have no idea. I hope, I pray that Pierre can keep us together. What will I do in a strange foreign place, all alone? If they take him, where will we go, how will we protect ourselves?

So many people have died. There are only a few whole families left. Young mothers have survived their older husbands. A band of four young boys races about, all of them orphans on the voyage. And then I see our neighbors: Annette and Roy, pale and weak, but alive and with their little girl, Marie, and their new baby alive also.

Annette comes over to me, holding her new baby, who is screaming now, over her shoulder. "Rose, do you know anything about what is to happen to us?" she asks.

"Nothing, Annette, except that we think that we are coming into New York."

"I hope we can stay together," she says. "I don't know if I can live to raise this child. I'm so weak." Deep lines etch her oval face, curving down her cheeks near her mouth, making her face like an old woman's. Brown and dull, the eyes that peer out of her thin face hold little hope for the future.

"God willing, we will stay together", I say in the most confident voice that I can manage. I reach out for her baby. He's like a feather in my arms. And I wonder, silently, if he will live.

"Can you speak any English, Rose?" Annette asks. "I know not a word. How will we get along without words in this new country?"

I shake my head, "I don't know." We both sigh, and then, realizing that I'm still holding the dear baby, I hand her over to Roy, and Annette and I fall into each other's arms. She is weeping again.

"Annette," I say as I step back, "the only thing that I've thought of that might win relief from brutal hard work, is to say that we can cook. Perhaps then we'd be in a kitchen where we can cook, and be around food that we might take for our families. That's all I can think of now."

Annette looks at me, "That's a good idea. We could keep our little one's with us, then." She goes on, "Of course we know... when you think of it... many tasks; weaving, planting, candle making, knitting ... It'll be easier on us if we don't get put to heavy field tasks."

"I brought a fricot pan with me," I half-smile, "not that I'm half as good as Maman at it, but I hope to get better."

A deep voice booms into my ears. "The English made us leave Acadia to get our good farms and land for themselves," Roy says. "I don't think they care how we get along." Then he stops speaking, as he sees the fear in Annette's tired face.

I tell them, "Marie Josèphe knows some English. We hope to stay together whatever happens. We will try to help you and your family if we can."

Roy puts his arm around Annette's shoulder. Annette's smile lights her face and almost makes her look young again. I smile at her. Then I turn to the ship's rail, a prayer on my lips.

Most stand on deck looking out at the many ships beating up the Harbor the same way that we are. Then I feel a hand tugging at my skirt.

"The sailors let me climb the low rigging," Jacques crows, his dark eyes dancing in his ruddy cheeks. "We are near land. I saw it!". "What are we going to do now, Rose? When we get off the ship, will Maman be waiting for us? And Madeleine, will she be here too?"

Jacques's eyes are bright and full of hope, as he tugs at my hand and points to the rolling hills we now sail past; green fields where cattle graze. "Look, Rose! Green fields. Soon, we will be in our new home!"

Oh my God. What to say. But I need not say encouraging things to Jacques. His sunny ways help him to see the bright side of things, without my words.

Pierre slowly walks over and gives Jacques a playful punch to the shoulder. "So, you have become a sailor, eh? Maybe we should leave you behind on the boat, eh?"

Jacques's face fades from sun to shadow in an instant. "Pierre! I want to be with you!" He looks guiltily at me, "and of course, you, Rose."

"Jacques, stay close, so that we will be together, whatever happens," I say firmly but have to smile at his excitement, even still.

Marie Josèphe looks at Pierre. "May I stay with you, too?" she asks.

Pierre hugs her. "But yes!" He turns to me, "Rose, I've no idea what will happen when we land. Please God some other Acadians are here already, who can help us."

My heart leaps at his words: Maman, Madeleine, André, people from our village put on other ships will they be here? But then hope fades. Marie Josèphe has heard sailors say that we may be the first ship to unload Acadians in this place.

CHAPTER TWELVE

THE QUILTS

Unfamiliar as this ship was, strangely, it will be hard to leave it. Horrible as it was for us, it is now familiar.

To go off with unknown people to unknown places, terrifies me. Now we face an unknown place and strange people. We who have come from a place where most of our lives were spent working in our homes or on our farms or sailing on our Acadian boats, we have little knowledge of living in other places. Yes, a few of us travelled to the southern islands for trade or within northern North America or to Europe for trade reasons but most of us had little to do with living anywhere else than Acadia. Now we will have to live in a new world where people speak their own words that we don't understand. And these new people may not understand me.

Never have I felt so alone. The desperate sense that I am without all the support of our Acadian friends, family, community and church, settles upon me… We Acadians have been harshly up-rooted. I have lost my Papa, my Maman and my little sister.

But I will go on, I will go on, if we must learn to exist in a new place, I will do it, but I will never give up my Acadian spirit. And I will never give up praying, hoping to find Madeleine and Maman.

In Acadia, we Acadians had some good friends that were English. I pray that we, my little group, can find some people like that in New York, some English people who think that we were unjustly persecuted and will try to help us, maybe even help us escape. But who knows if that will happen?

The curly-haired sailor now slips behind us and whispers for us to get our things from the hold. We start a bit before the others and I find my little trunk, my sac with my cooking pot and our quilt. We are just coming out when the crowd goes down to get their things.

"I hid my Maman's combs behind a timber and forgot to take them out," Marie Josèphe says with a worried look.

"I'll go back with you, "Pierre says. "And Rose, did you lock your little trunk?"

"I did," I say, as I watch the sailors carrying out small chests and tables and larger trunks that some passengers packed away so long ago. I see piles of quilts dumped on the deck and Marie Josèphe rushes forward to look for her quilt, and I rush forward to look for the other quilts we brought.

But we are held back. As we stand, penned in by sailors, the quilts are piled on a spare sail, carried down the gangplank and put on the pier. Then boys run up with flaming torches and set them on fire.

Roy and Annette's new quilt, my quilt, everyone's quilt: my heart curls up like a worm; it feels as if it is touched with a flame as well. We are so beaten down. Only quilts, could the English not have allowed us to keep these precious possessions?

"It is because of smallpox that the quilts are burned," the curly-haired sailor says in French. "The officials here fear smallpox will kill their citizens. We cannot land unless these things are burned."

I look at the pile of burning quilts which the men have bolstered with dry wood. Soon, all the quilts are reduced to ashes. I have only my clothes, my little bird, *Espère*, the things in my small trunk, my leather sac, and my cooking pot to remind me of home in Acadia.

On the wharf, carts are pulled up in a tremendous clatter. The men who drive ox or single horse carts wear pants to the knee and loose, billowing shirts and large floppy hats.

We watch them and they watch us. No one is sure; no one seems to know what is to become of us. Then, we hear shouts and the rattle and rumble of horses and carriages on cobblestones. We see a carriage, filled with men dressed in uniforms.

Pierre tells us, "Perhaps the English will announce their plans for us now. Listen carefully."

An open carriage, surrounded by British soldiers, on horseback, races onto the wharf. The coach comes to a clattering halt. Two British officers jump down. Two barrels are set on end, and two soldiers climb on top of them. A horn blows shrill and loud.

The people on the dock first look at them and then look with curiosity at us, and then begin to mutter and yell at us. The soldiers quiet them with cocked muskets.

We hear one officer read from a paper in poor French.

"The Governor of New York decrees that these newly arrived French Neutrals, lately from Acadia, are dangerous enemies in our midst. They refused to honor the British Crown and may try to start a battle for the French Cause. These people could be dangerous. Beware of them, they and their Indian allies have killed many of our citizens."

Marie Josèphe, in a low voice, explains some words. What now? Our burned quilts still burn on the pier. Must we climb into empty wagons with no idea where the wagons will take us? Can we stay together? I clutch Jacques's hand tight but feel my legs tremble.

"*Allons, en famille,*" I whisper. Our little group, Pierre and Marie Josèphe, Jacques and I walk down the gangplank to leave The Experiment. We'll now find out whatever lies ahead.

I breathe deeply and pray an Our Father to help us. Along with the others, we stand on the wharf. A blond fellow about Pierre's age and, an old man, walk up to the guard watching us. The old man speaks to the guard, drops some coins in his hand and shows him a piece of paper. Then he moves his musket from lying across his shoulder into both of his hands. He points it at us.

Bravely, Marie Josèphe steps out, says, "*Pardon Monsieur,*" and then speaks a few English words, pointing to our small trunks and bags and begs permission to get our things. He answers curtly. Finally, I find my little trunk and my sac with the cooking pot handle sticking out. We have to follow the man. We look for Annette and Roy, but we have lost them.

"NOOO," a desperate scream rings out from behind, from Annette, and I try to run back to her, but the man's gun is in my face. Oh my g... What could have happened? Oh, the poor woman and family, God help them now!

Marie Josèphe and I look at each other and there is no word to be said. As Papa said, it seems like years ago, "We are… truly… lost,"

That night we spend with our legs chained, lying on the dirt floor of a hut near the riverbank. In the morning, the old man cracks the locked door open of our hut and steps inside. "YOU! ACADIANS!" He shouts in a loud voice. "STAND!"

We stagger to stand, stiff and confused, and look at him. With his left hand he drags a sack. "Bread!" he says gruffly. Behind him a young man walks into our hut carrying two thin water pots, slung on each side of his slender frame.

The man we see is the same yellow-haired fellow we saw yesterday. Now he walks around and unlocks our foot shackles. With a musket in his arm, he watches us gnaw the bread and drink the water with our shackled hands, and then waves to us to follow him. Outside, he unshackles our hands and points to a hut that smells of body waste. He sits down and waits with his musket while one by one we use it.

Pointing his gun again, and not speaking, he herds us in front of him like sheep and points for us to walk down the grassy slope towards the water. Our bones aching and our heads dizzy, we stumble and slide down the muddy bank.

Pierre mutters in my ear, "We could attack him easily. But then what... no one here, no way to freedom." Jacques half slides, half runs ahead, excited for he sees another boat to ride in. A large ship's boat bounces in gentle waves a few yards offshore. The boat has a main sail and then a small front sail.

The boy points to it, and gestures that we should wade in the water and climb aboard. He holds his musket loosely as we move forward.

The old man in the boat grabs Marie Josèphe's hand and hauls her into the boat like a sack of wheat. He seats her mid boat on one side. He sends the younger man back for our bundles and places the rest of us: me, beside Marie Josèphe, Jacques in front of the old man, in the front tip of the boat, Pierre behind the boy-sailor who sails the boat. Using a stick, the boy poles us away from the shore and into deeper water and begins to raise a sail.

To go where?

CHAPTER THIRTEEN

HELL-GUT

It's a large river we are in, filled with small and large sailing craft. Along the side of us are large ships now anchored at the City of New York. We see behind the ships, buildings and people walking about and cargo being unloaded from the ships. We have heard of the Port of New York and now, we are in the midst of it. But not to stay.

The boy raises the sail. We seem to be heading along the shore of the river.

A hand pokes my shoulder. I take the hunk of bread Marie Josèphe saved for me. I stuff the whole piece in my mouth. It is dry but my weakness goes away as I get the food in my stomach.

Suddenly, I feel myself nearly in the water. Marie Josèphe has tried to lunge off the boat. I grab for her as the side of the boat dips hard to the side. Pierre reaches past me grabs her long hair and pulls hard. She screams and falls back into the boat. Stunned, she turns towards me, on her arm is a red welt where it hit the side of the boat. "*Stupide!*" I snap. "Pierre loves you. We all need you." She leans against me, and sobs shake her body.

The boy skillfully pulls a rope that raises the main sail, and then the small sail. He points to my head and indicates that I must duck when the sail swings about.

Across from us are still buildings and ships tied up at piers. But the boy gradually tacks to turn away from the buildings and wharves. He sails the boat on a path away from the deep Harbor and alongside the river. We glide peacefully upriver.

"Marie Josèphe, see the fields and the cows," I say. "And the children fishing from the shore. Like home, yes?" Marie Josèphe doesn't answer. We sail quietly along the riverbanks…

Then, our boat suddenly jerks and races perilously fast, carried by currents of the water. I look at the boy at the helm. Sweat trickles down his taut face. His eyes race back and forth between the water and the rocks. The old man calls out signals, telling him to steer one way or the other.

"Aiyee!" Marie Josèphe screams. The boat seems to be caught in a whirlpool and spins. But then it shoots ahead. Foamy current swirls around us. Huge rocks jut up suddenly and the boy slams the rudder hard to get away from them. Marie Josèphe screams with every breath.

I shout and clutch Jacques. It's still a bright, spring day, with gulls sweeping leisurely overhead and the lands on the sides of the water quiet and peaceful, filled with livestock and trees unbent with the wind.

But, still, our boat spins and dips as if it will sink to the depths of the river. Huge, jagged rocks jut out near our boat and the sloop in front. The waters boil like the devil has stirred a pot of boiling oil. A new powerful wave pushes us straight ahead towards more savage rocks.

"Hell-got," I hear the boy cry. Marie Josèphe and I cry out, "*Notre Dame, Sainte Jeanne*" to help us. Then as we get through the rocks, the water calms. We are still so terrified that we clasp hands together and continue to pray quietly.

Working the rudder and the sail rope, the blond young man steadies our boat. We sail quietly, tacking back and forth until soon, we are in a large, pleasant bay, with the sails of small and fishing craft boats all around us.

I slump back and breathe a sigh of relief. The old man speaks to us. Now that it is quiet, I notice that his eyes are mossy green, like the stream near our home in Belle Isle. I cannot understand his words, but I sense that he is now trying to be kind.

Marie Josèphe watches his mouth and listens carefully, "I think he is saying that we will sail onward for

a day or so but for us to be prepared to sleep in sheds if we
have to land, he'll do his best."

I am weary, so weary and stiff and hungry. Will this
voyage ever end?

Finally, as dusk falls, the boat leaves the large bay.
We enter a smaller bay and can see lights glowing through
the windows of a few scattered houses in the forests beside
the water. Water slaps against the hull of the boat. A full
moon hangs in the sky. Ahead I can make out boats
clustered near shore.

Finally, cold, wet, and sleepy, we stand on the planks
of a dock. We hear the water sloshing gently around under
us. The moon's light is hidden on and off by clouds that
slip over the moon.

The old man shakes a wooden club at us. The boy
who sailed with us from New York City says quietly in
French, "Do not try to run. There is nowhere for you to
go."

This is how I feel. I have no idea where I could run
and hide in this dark night.

We stand beside the bundles that the yellow-haired
boy has brought up from the boat while the old man talks
to a person who seems to guard the docks. The person
turns and walks to a fishing boat tied up but with sails still

up. While we catch our breath, the old man tells us to sit for a moment and we are glad to do it.

Jacques, half asleep, sits in front of me on the wharf. Pierre holds Marie Josèphe in his arms as they rest.

Then three burly men walk towards us. Half asleep as I am, they remind me of big, strong fisherman from Annapolis Royal: their steps rock slightly. But, as I turn to talk to Jacques, Pierre bellows like a mad bull.

The men have rushed at Pierre, grabbed him, thrown sails over his head, thrown a rope around him and dragged him away. Marie Josèphe who has fallen backward and hit her head takes a minute to know what has happened.

Pierre yells, "Marie Josèphe, Rose, Jacques!" I hear rough male voices and then, they are gone. Silence. Jacques screams and runs after them, off into the night.

Still dizzy from the blow to her head, Marie Josèphe says, plaintively, "We are alone."

Jacques sits like a stone on the dock. Tears pour down his cheeks.

"Did you hear where they were going?" I ask Jacques.

Marie Josèphe reaches out and puts her hand on my arm. She shakes her head. "They are gone. I heard them bellowing and calling, and then, I think that I heard a boat's sails flapping back and forth and then… silence. I don't know. I don't know," she wails the last words.

Marie Josèphe hears something.

She turns to me and whispers, "The boy says that Pierre is taken to work on fishing boats. He does not know where."

I try to get my feet and legs underneath me so I can move quickly. It is better to do something to escape our fate, than nothing. I wave at my friend to follow me and grab Jacques's hand and stride off: dragging him down the dock.

The old man sees me. He shouts. The yellow-haired boy runs after us and grabs Jacques. "Don't run," he says to me in French, "I have the boy." The old man catches up to us and his gun forces us to climb into a horse-drawn wagon. The wagon jerks forward and collapsing, I faintly hear the clip-clops of the horse.

We need Pierre now! That was my brother they stole for their damn fishing boats.

Marie Josèphe crouches beside me in the hay. It is her beloved that they have stolen… "Maybe we can overcome him," she whispers, nodding towards the old man.

I am strong, in spirit at least. Gathering my strength, I stand, pick up a staff left in the hay, swing it, and knock the driver off his perch. Somehow, I will go back and find Pierre. I do not know how, but I will. The old man rises, strong enough to resist. He pulls the horse to a stop, grabs the staff from me and swings it back at me.

When I wake, blood is caked on my cheek. Violent pain throbs in my ear. I feel weak, bruised, and shaken. I must learn not just to act but to plan ahead. We must be quite far from the dock where we landed. The wagon jounces along. I don't want to open my eyes. What difference does it make where we are?

But soon, day breaks. A soft breeze brushes my cheek and overhead I see clouds drifting in the blue sky. It feels like a spring day and I cannot resist the sense of hope that early spring always brings to me. I struggle to sit up. "Where are we?"

"*Je ne sais pas,*" Marie Josèphe says with a wry grin, "Are you all right? He hit you so hard. And then you just dropped. I didn't know what to do but finally thought it best to let you sleep as you were breathing."

She holds with one arm to the side of the wagon. Her other hand loosely rests on Jacques' sleeping body where he sprawls on the hay. Birds chatter in the bushes.

A moment of last night comes back to me. I reach out to touch Marie Josèphe. Softly, I ask, "What did the boy say to you, when Pierre was snatched away?"

She puts a finger to her lips, nodding towards the old man. Painfully, I move closer to her.

"He said that Pierre would work on a fishing boat that sails out of "Promised Land.""

A tiny bit of hope springs up in me. I do not know why he decided to tell us this, but it may be helpful, and I'm glad he did. I close my eyes and think quietly. What would Papa do if he was in our shoes? I look down at the battered wooden shoes, my sabots that I still wear though my feet have grown. I won't be able to wear them much longer.

Papa would try to figure out a way to make things go our way. It seems impossible, but still… we must never give up.

What do I know that could help us later? I know that New York Harbor has ships that come and go to far distant lands. That is good to know.

If, somehow, we all can find our way back to New York, we might get on a ship to Acadia or somewhere else that is French land, and, perhaps, we might find Maman and André and Madeleine who might return there if they are able to… NO, I gulp. This doesn't make sense.

I turn back to Marie Josèphe. "Let's try to stay together, no matter what happens, "I say.

"*Oui*," she says dully.

Jacques stirs and opens his dark eyes. I gently take hold of his skinny hands and pull him upright. "Where are we?" he mumbles. I take him on my lap and prop him up so that he can see over the sides of the cart.

"So, Jacques, we are on an adventure," I say confidently. "You will have a good tale to tell Oncle Louis, when we see him. Nearly as good as his *voyageur* tales. Yes?" I try to make him smile.

Jacques looks at me again. The sorrow in his eyes. He has seen his father buried at sea, his mother carried off on a strange ship, and his brother taken off in the night.

I hug his skinny chest to mine. Then set him gently back in the hay. He turns those eyes to me again, and asks, "Pierre. Where is he?"

"Your brother is on a fishing boat," I say. "You know, like the ones that docked in Annapolis Harbor. We will make a game to guess how many days, till he comes home."

Jacques' head lifts and his voice brightens. "What do I get if I win?"

"I'll give you the shiny fish hook that I put in my bag," says Marie Josèphe.

"Ten days," Jacques says.

"We will wait and see," I tell him.

His head drops so that his black hair falls across his face as he falls back to sleep. I shift his body onto the hay and sit at the side of the wagon looking out. The land here is flat. There are no mountains or even hills such as we had in Acadia. A forest with sturdy tall trees lines both sides of the road. After a while, cleared fields spread beside the road. Some fields are plowed and sprouting with green.

Spring in Belle Isle was apple trees in blossom, seeds in Maman's garden and lambs about the fields. Quietly, little pieces of my life float back into my head, I want to hold onto them forever. The Saturday mornings, when relieved from work, we might wander with our boy and girl friends in Annapolis Royal, visiting André's father's shop, catching up on all the gossip, and after coming back to Belle Isle, gathering together again for a dancing party. What fun it was... and Sunday's after Church, often visiting with our older family and later walking in our apple orchards.

Night times were for stories, I see Maman at her spinning wheel and all of us sprawled about near the fire, listening to Oncle Etienne spin his fantastic tales of kings and knights in France or the Mi'kmaq tales of Glooscap, the great spirit of their tribe.

Quietly, I remember them. And I will always remember them, to keep up my spirit. But now, it is too sad.

Here now, I shake my head to clear it and instead, when a person walks or drives by, I try to see past their clothes, homespun shirts and pants and woven hats into the very people themselves. There must be kind people here. There must be.

The driver stops where a gate crosses the road, and he seems to pay the gate keeper for us to continue down the road.

"Acadians!" The man calls to us as we continue our journey. "Food."

He throws back a dripping cheese tangy with spring onion and a loaf of bread.

The rich, sloppy cheese reminds me of the little stone milk house at our Farm where Papa dammed spring to store our butter and milk and cheeses. Tears rise. But I look at Marie Josèphe and she is tearing into the bread onto which she has placed a hunk of dripping cheese.

She smiles with her mouth full. "This the best food in…," a shocked look crosses her now thinner face. "How long?" She stammers. "How long is it since this journey began that brings us here?"

"T'was cold when we were put on the boats in Annapolis Royal," Jacques pipes up around a mouthful of bread and cheese.

"Ah, yes," Marie Josèphe says, "it was Our Lady's Day, December 8th, when we left Acadia forever."

"Not forever," I say quietly, "We must never say that."

"And now, it feels like April," I say wonderingly. "Perhaps it is three months since we left home in Nova Scotia. Those awful days at sea, having to wait in Antiqua, while the ship was repaired from the hurricane damage... We speak in French in low tones; the rattle and clatter of the wagon masking our words

"I heard some words on the dock in New York City that Acadian young or old might be indentured servants. I don't know what that means. And I don't know what will happen to us," Marie Josèphe says. "Will we be put to work in these fields? Will they treat us like animals, and keep us in the barn?"

She drops her face between her slim hands. "I never worked in the fields at home. Maman and Papa were so old that they mostly just lived from their vegetable garden and the fish, especially the salmon, Papa could catch in the river."

"*Mon Dieu*, I pray that we can stay together," I say. "Remember the Acadian sisters on the wharf? One went off in a fancy carriage. The other in a farm cart? I pray that doesn't happen to us,"

The wagon jounces along. My head aches worse than before. "Hallo!" Jacques calls out as the cart goes over a bump and he wakes up again. "Where are we now?"

Marie Josèphe calls to the driver in English, "*Monsieur*, where are we?"

The cart driver roughly bangs his whip on the side of the cart to make his horse step out at a brisk trot. Speaking slowly in English, he says, "This is the village of East Hampton, your new home."

Never! I think. But I sit up and look around.

CHAPTER FOURTEEN

OUR NEW VILLAGE

The cart turns, runs along beside a pond, and nearby is a green field with cows grazing in it. There are rows of houses lined up facing the pond. I smell wood smoke with food in its curls from the house chimneys. I'm so hungry.

In a moment, a fresh salty breeze tells me we are near the sea and as I look about, I guess that perhaps, somewhere behind the houses, is the ocean. For a moment, I stand shakily and yes, I can see the ocean glimmering in the sun. Behind the houses are long, narrow lots that reach away, probably to the ocean.

Jacques looks about with his eager eyes, for water, for he loves ships, but he is too small yet to see the ocean far behind the houses. "Maybe Pierre will be here," He says hopefully, "I can smell the sea."

There are small buildings about near the pond and green. That is all I know now.

"Rose, look!" Jacques says. Little children, laughing and pointing, are running barefoot beside our cart. He sees the children as friends to play with. But I'm not so sure. A little boy aims a make-believe musket at us.

The driver pulls his horse to a stop, comes back and drops the side of the cart. He jerks Jacques roughly out of the cart onto the ground. Marie Josèphe and I climb down. The man drops our trunks beside the wagon. My trunk cracks and a corner splits. I try to pick it up. The driver heaves my sac with my cooking pot in the air and it drops with a thud. But when I get my arms around some of my things, I am too weak to lift them. I stand up and stumble on the rutted dirt road. Marie Josèphe grabs my hand, "Together," she whispers.

"*Oui*," I say, "There are so many people around us. We must stay together."

We three are pushed away from the road and into the middle of a circle of people. They are probably farmers, I think. I don't see clothes trimmed with lace and hats with flowers like I did in New York City. But I see a few men, not dressed as farmers, but in dark clothes, perhaps preachers. One man with the brown skin and long black hair of a native person is in the crowd, but he is dressed not in leather and feathers but shabby farmer clothes.

There's a questioning look in the eyes of these people. Their eyes stare at us. The people chatter back and forth much as we might have, if strange people were brought to our village.

A man holds up a paper, reads from it, points at us. The people start to mutter and cast us angry glances.

Marie Josèphe says behind her hand. "The man said that their English King has declared war against France. These people think that we are French and that we may fight or spy for the French. Some of them look angry."

"*Non, pas Français!*" I say loudly. Marie Josèphe speaks out in English. No one listens to her. The people are too excited about thinking that we are enemies. They frown and their eyes are cold as they look at us.

A big boy grabs Jacques and laughing, drags him across the green into the pond at the end of the village green.

Jacques comes back, crying, with mud on his stockings and breeches. Wiping his tears away, I stoop down and hug him. "It'll all right, Jacques. I'll take care of you."

His brown eyes doubt me. He wipes tears away and stands a bit away from me.

Now the people in the circle talk loudly. I look to Marie Josèphe to tell me what a young blond man announces in a loud voice. She tells me, "We must go to their church. We may not speak French, we must speak English. Jacques must work as an apprentice. He cannot stay with you. He may not even stay in this village. And we must work as servants but not with the same family."

"*Non!*" I cry and look around for Jacques. At that moment, a man reaches by me and grabs him. The man throws Jacques's thin body over his shoulder like a balky calf as Jacques screams and kicks his feet. His screams tear out pieces of my heart. The man plunges ahead through the cows and townsfolk on the green, heading for a path at the far end of the green. I have a desperate sense that Jacques is going to disappear forever as all the others have.

"Jacques! I'm coming!"

I jump-start and run faster than the people chasing me. Loud shouts sound in my ears. My head's down and I run smack into a body: a man with his arms outstretched like a gate.

"Stop! Stop!" he says in good French. His strong arms clutch me. We are alone in the middle of the path when he leans over and says in French, "I am the teacher here, Master Wells, I will help you and the boy. Now, you must go back."

He pushes me to turn around. I stumble back to the village green and the villagers crowd around me. People so close to me scare me. I back up. But they are behind me and in front of me. I drop my head and don't look at anyone.

Stepping forward quickly, a man marches up to me and shoves my shoulder, "French, eh?" he spits the words in my face.

"*Non*," I say to whatever he says and stamp my foot and glare at him.

A loud cry from the far side of the green startles him and the man steps back. The circle around me opens and I see Marie Josèphe. She stands beside a stout woman with hair yellow as straw. As Marie Josèphe sees me, she crashes through the people around her and runs to me. Tears streak her dirty face.

"Rose!" she screams. "They take me away." Her eyes blink very fast. The muscles in her face twitch as though she is having a fit.

Reaching out for her, I hold her close to me, to feel her, to have her feel my arms around her. Even though I am smaller than she, I pull her body towards mine. The people around me must pity her for they stand back.

Slowly, she speaks; half weeping and talking. "Rose. I go away with those people. I go away."

I stroke her back, hug her again. "You'll be all right," I whisper in French. "Pray! We will be together again." I look into her troubled eyes. I put my arm on her shoulder, but she pulls away and walks back across the green alone: a drooping figure in ragged clothes.

My heart sinks. Now, I am alone. Desperately, I look for a kind face and see no one. My body trembles and my mind freezes and my knees give way under me.

I wake on the ground. A woman's face floats over me. She is fair skinned with green eyes. She tries to raise me from the ground, "Up! You must get up!"

I know what she means but I close my eyes say "*Non*," and inside, stiffen my will to resist her, or anyone English.

"You must get up!" Water trickles down my face. I look up. From a bowl the woman holds she sprinkles more water on my face. I am groggy and look around for Jacques or Marie Josèphe or Pierre. No one.

Inside, I try to strengthen my spirit. I draw a deep breath. I've done nothing wrong. Why are these people yelling at me?

"Come!" The bearded, stocky man tries to pull me after him.

"*Non!*" I shake my head. A few of the people who still stand about shout English words. They look at me and talk to each other as if I had done a terrible thing.

"Abigail," the stocky man bellows at the red-haired woman who dropped water on my face.

"Yes, Jonas," she answers. I see now that she is a small frail woman, big with child.

"Abigail," he jerks his thumb upwards, says some English words and points at me.

Abigail stands up slowly because of her big belly. She holds out her hand, and I take it and shakily stand.

The teacher-man speaks out. "What is your name, girl? We must know that" the teacher asks me in French.

"Rose," I say, "Rosalie from Belle-Isle."

"Rose," he repeats.

The teacher man speaks English now but the way he speaks, firm and like a teacher, stops my new Master, Jonas.

Then the teacher begins to speak to me. He speaks French quickly. His French is different from our Acadian French. I do not understand everything. Often, the teacher asks because I must look stupid, "Do you understand?"

"*Un peu*," I say.

"It is good that you understand a little," the teacher says. He speaks more slowly.

I hear again what Marie Josèphe thought she heard that I must work as a house servant.

"But Jacques, what will happen to my little brother?" I say to the teacher in French.

A worried look flashed over his face. "I'm not sure, I'll try to find out."

"*S'il vous plait, Maître,*" I drop to my knees and say in French.

"Please, take care of him," I beg. Then I feel tears starting but I quickly wipe them away and turn to walk towards my little trunk, abandoned by the roadside. This I must have, I think: my last little bit of home.

The teacher-man stops me. "I'm not finished," he says, with a sad look on his face. "There are rules for 'French aliens,' as you are called. First: you may not speak French. All Acadians must learn and use English." He stops talking and takes a deep breath.

I look at him to see what he will say next.

"Rose," he says in a gentle voice, his eyes on mine, saying something, but I do not know what. He raises his voice and speaks clearly, "Second: the Governor has ordered: all Acadians must go to our church services here…"

Teacher-man holds up three fingers, "Third: the little boy may be sent to another village. I hear word from the men in town that an old weaver in another Village has sent out word, he needs an apprentice."

"NO! He's too young to be alone, NO!"

The teacher shakes his head, hies eyes catch mine in a firm glance as he says quietly in French, "I cannot make that decision, but I'll do what I can, Rose." Then the teacher takes my arm gently and turns me towards the woman who tried to get me up. "Go," he says. "Mistress Abigail is near her birth-time. She is in needs of help. I will give you news of your little brother when I get it."

CHAPTER FIFTEEN

MEETING MASTER

The sun is now high overhead. Most of the villagers have gone off to their homes. I cannot run. I do not know where I am. I pick up my little trunk in both my arms, holding it against my chest, and turn toward the woman.

The woman, Abigail, tells a big boy to take my trunk and my sac with the cooking pot, to "Master Jonas's house".

"*C'est bien*, Rose," she says. She stands in front of me then. She looks around for Jonas, then speaks softly in French, looking in my eyes to see if I understand her words. "You'll work for us," she adds. I lift my head, look at her and listen.

Slowly, I nod my head because my spirit is near dead. I need to know what lies ahead and what will happen to Jacques. Abigail waves for me to follow her. Her two little girls race ahead. Her husband goes off to speak in a group of men. My feet ache in my wooden sabots, as I walk behind her. As I follow, I see that Abigail wears leather moccasins. Are there many native peoples near here I wonder?

Then, Abigail turns and slowly asks in French, "The boy. Is he your brother?"

"*Oui*." Hope springs up in my heart at Abigail's interest.

Abigail starts walking again, breathing heavily in the moist mid-morning sunlight. She points for me to walk beside her. "Soon, we go see boy," she says. "He stays with carpenter in this village." She makes a motion of sawing and hammering. "But, he may leave here," she adds. The sound of her voice drops as if she doesn't want me to hear what she says.

"*Non*!" To lose Jacques would be to lose... everything... my family, my joy. "*Non*!" I shout.

"Rose," she murmurs, "my husband said, not me."

The woman's two little girls chase geese on the green, and Abigail calls them back. She points to one, "Lydia," she says, pointing at the dark-haired one with braids, who makes a face at me, and "Phoebe," the other; red haired and freckle faced, who smiles shyly, under her mob cap.

The two are little girls, just a little older than Madeleine. They don't know about all the heartbreak I feel, so I take the younger one, Phoebe's, hand. We walk at the edge of the broad green space in the village where cattle and sheep graze. Past more houses, and a cemetery. At the bottom of a gentle hill, Abigail opens a gate in a fence. She says, "*Notre Maison.*" In front of me is a house different from ours in Acadia. It seems to have two levels in front of the house, and one in the back. The roof in the back slides down like a hill. There's a garden beside the house; the plants seem to blow in the wind, a little less tidy than our garden at home, I trip on the big flat stone in front of the house door, fall and cut my knee.

"Sit!" Abigail quickly says and points to the step. She comes back with a cool wet cloth and wipes my knee. Lydia takes my hand and tries to pull me up. But she is too little, and I am too weak. We both laugh a little at her trying to get a big person to stand up. I finally stagger up myself. Lydia giggles and runs away. Even though my knees are weak from sitting for so much in the boat and in the cart, I am curious to see how these people live. Already I see that this home is more like André's house in the village of Annapolis Royal than our home in the country.

Inside the front door, steps go straight up, and on one side a room has sturdy wooden benches, a rag rug, one chair and a small table which has on it, a few pottery bowls and perhaps a candle stand. The front hall windows beside me let in light and there is a thick rag rug in front of the stairs. On the other side of the stairway is a room with a large loom, a spinning wheel, piles of sheep fleeces and small benches scattered about. Wisps of wool lie on the floor.

Abigail calls me into the kitchen in the back of the house behind the stairs and the chimney. A light spring breeze ruffles the short curtains in the kitchen. The smells of freshly plowed earth and cow manure and salt blows into the house.

Tears choke my throat. That light breeze could be a breeze in my own home.

Abigail calls, "Rose! Come!"

I stand, clenching my fingers. What a strange voice. I want to hear my own Maman's voice calling me. Anger surges in my chest. How could the English tear us Acadians all out of our dear homes and abandon us to strange people and strange places?

As I move into the kitchen, the smell of a banked fire and fresh baked bread fills my nose. The kitchen has a large hearth with several black pots hanging over the fire and a bread oven to the side. Just now her husband, Maître Jonas, bangs open the back door of the kitchen. He has to stoop to get in, this part of the house is low and warm. Another spinning wheel, more sheep fleeces strewn about and a simple board table, benches and two chairs fill the room.

Jonas stares at me, then goes directly through the kitchen into the loom room. Abigail points for me to sit on a bench and busies herself with stirring whatever is in a black pot. I hear the noise of the loom clicking back and forth. Mistress Abigail soon calls out for the family to come to eat.

Master comes over and sits on a bench at the rough table with the two little girls. Abigail serves the hot dish from the black pot into one bowl. I'm not asked to eat. Fainting with hunger, I watch while the family eats warm bread dipped into steaming mush in their wooden bowls. When the family finishes, Abigail calls me to the table and gives me a wooden bowl of golden mush. Just as I lift the bowl to my lips, little Lydia cries out "Mama, more!" and grabs my bowl.

Starved as I am, I snatch for the bowl myself. But the bowl slips from my hand and falls on the stones of the hearth. Mush splatters everywhere, on the spinning wheel, the raw wool, the black pot.

"What's this?" Master Jonas shouts, his face reddened with anger. Abigail pours what little food is left in the black pot into the bowl. I upend it and swallow it. I am still starved.

Master Jonas stands up. In seconds, he is in front of me. His brown eyes seem to scorch me, his lips drawn back to show his crooked teeth. Then, he walks out the back door. The door latch shakes and opens again.

A person with black skin walks into the kitchen. I stare at her. I have heard of such people. I look away and look back again. She's a small black girl and her eyes don't meet mine. She glances at me for a moment then looks at the floor as though this is the way she always meets people. She carries an armload of firewood and stacks it beside the hearth. Then she looks at Mistress and says a few words softly. A bowl of food is given to her, and she takes it not to the table but to a little stool set in the corner where she sits and slurps it up. She has no spoon.

The thought comes: she is a Negro slave. I had heard that in the English colonies, black people from Africa are bought and sold and kept as slaves.

Will I be a slave, here, too? I have heard that these people are beaten and chained. Will that happen to me? I steal another look at the slave girl, to see signs of ill-use on her body. It is sad that I am not thinking of her, but of what may happen to me. I am ashamed, but I cannot help it.

The black girl is hushed in her ways. Abigail looks gravely at her and points to her to clean the pot she has used. The girl reaches into a basket of sand, dumps it into the pot and scrubs.

I am trying to get the food mess that spilled from my samp bowl out of a basket of sheared wool when I half notice the creak of the door opening again. I keep picking away trying to get the wool fibers clean of the gold mash when a strong hand from behind grabs my shoulder.

"You! Come with me!" the Master says in a low voice. Such short words I understand. What will he do to me? He takes me outside. I am so terrified that I wet myself.

He points to tell me what to do. I must pick up a tall log with a rounded end and pound dried corn kernels in a hollowed-out bowl log, until they break down into mush. Soon, my shoulders stab with pain.

Then, Master brings me back into the house and directs me to carry a heavy kettle of hot water back and forth to a barrel outside where I must scrub large sheets with soft soap then wring them out as I can and hang them on the back fence. Finally, I look at him, raise my hands and shake my head.

Leaning against an apple tree, he watches me, smiles slowly, and nods up and down.

"*Non,*" I say boldly looking at him, "*C'est fini.*" And I quake inside wondering if he will punish me for my bold words. He shakes his head, but he stops giving me orders. I'm glad I spoke out. There are times when being bold helps me. He turns now and walks away.

Mistress Hanna, who comes into the yard as well, tells her little girls to pick up the dragging ends of the last sheet so they do not soil from the dirt. But she does not help me.

It is dusk now, and I hear birds twittering as they seek the barn. Exhausted as I am I can't even walk straight but Jonas takes me into a shed to milk his cow. Even the things that I did do at home for my mother are hard for me now. My legs tremble, my head shoots with pain from my aching forehead. I am so tired, so weak, so confused and robbed of all hope.

I lug the filled wooden milk pail, sloshing with milk, back into the kitchen. Abigail says not a word of thanks to me. She lights a candle and walks with her two little girls to a straw mattress in a little side room off one side of the kitchen. There she hears their prayers, but I don't understand them. I breathe the prayers we said at nightfall in our own home in Acadia.

Remembering the young black girl, I look around and see that she stands behind me. Silently, she holds out a hunk of bread. I grab it and gnaw it like a dog. The girl points to herself and says, "Pegg," in a low voice. She moves her arm to show I should follow her, so I trudge up rough stairs into a low attic space, strung with dried apples. The apples' cidery smell reminds me of the attic at home in Acadia. Two thin blankets lie thrown on the floor in the corner. Pegg picks up one. She gives it to me.

Wrapping it around my shoulders, I lean on the window ledge. Stars flicker in the night sky; these stars shine tonight over Acadia too. And I remember what Papa told me about the way to find special stars and he told me stories about them.

Acadians are like stars scattered about the world, but only the English know where to find them. I don't.

Downstairs I hear the door crash shut and Jonas's rough voice call "Abigail!" I hear her singing to the little girls, to settle them in sleep. I hear a loud crash and the girls' startled cry. Abigail's soft voice hums now. Tears wet my cheeks. I think of my own, missing family. Madeleine, dear little Madeleine, is she alive? Where is my mother, Céline? Is she still alive? Somehow, I wish to gather our family together, like a hen gathers her chicks from far corners of the barnyard. But can I find them?

As I stare at the sky, I cannot think anymore of my family and friends. It is too sad. Sleep overcomes me and I reach for the beaver skin that always kept me warm in the night in Acadia. But no warm, furry skin touches my fingers. I clutch Pegg's thin, scratchy blanket.

I say to God angrily before I turn back to sleep. "I will never give up my search for freedom and my people. But I will not pray to you God. I will not pray to you tonight, God, because you are not there for me."

CHAPTER SIXTEEN

A NEW FRIEND?

In the morning, the birds chatter and sing so loud that I hear them inside the attic. A shadow flits across the attic window and then flits back. Is a bird nesting in the eaves? I think so. I hear a twitter of little hungry bird sounds. Groping in my pocket, I grasp the little wooden bird, the one that André gave me, the one I named *Espère*, because it gives me hope. After Jonas's harsh treatment yesterday, I need it.

Lying still, I close my eyes, and I am in Acadia with André. He leans over me in our canoe so that he can net the trout I have caught. He uses one arm to steady me and the other to sweep the fish into the boat. The smell of his sweat, his arms surround me. And then the fish flops wildly around the canoe. André gives the line a sharp jerk...when . . .

"Up!" the man's head is sticking into the attic. "Up!"

That man, Jonas, so strong with thickly muscled arms, I cannot resist for I don't know what he might do. Pegg is up already.

After Jonas leaves, I use the chamber pot; and as I straighten up I smell myself: filthy with sweat, toilet soil and now dirty clothes.

Feeling my greasy hair, I use the bone comb that Running Deer gave me. And the comb cracks and its teeth fall out. A feeling of utter sadness sweeps over me, not because of the broken comb exactly, but because the comb was a gift from Running Deer.

Now, she probably is up in the northern territories with her Mi'kmaq tribe. Her life goes on as always, I suppose; hunting and fishing in the summer, trapping for furs in the winter, tanning skins for leather.

But my life is not going forward in a straight line like hers. It's like a lightning-struck tree; it's split apart and could grow in any direction. Or die...

I slide across the hay to the ladder to the kitchen. As I half fall down the stairs, I see Abigail is sweeping the floor clean of mud and wool shreds. She waves at me and motions for me to sit. I eat the mush she puts in front of me, and my head isn't spinning anymore. Holding out my hand, I offer to take the broom from Abigail. But she shakes her head.

Abigail puts the broom in the corner and hands me a basin of water. She pulls on my chemise, and I understand that I am to take it off and wash it. Good. But after I put the basin down, she hands me the blouse I should wear, it's Jonas's.

I shake my head. "*Non.*" I cannot tell her the warning signs I feel. Abigail shakes her head, "*Oui,*" she says.

So, I take my filthy chemise and a wash basin into an alcove, put Jonas's shirt on and wash my own blouse. Jonas's shirt smells clean and feels soft. I am glad to wear it.

Then Jonas comes into the kitchen and sees me in his shirt. He growls, eyeing me with a black look. He strides across the room so that his face is inches from mine. I can see the spittle on his lips.

"Off!" he says to me, "Now." He pulls on the shirt, hard.

I hear Abigail protest. Then, Jonas growls words I don't understand, swings around and walks out the door. I untie the neck ribbons on Jonas's shirt, pull it over my head, walk over and take my wet blouse and put it on.

Without words to say in English, after I feel my own clammy chemise stick to my skin, I pound the table with my fist.

"Go outside," Abigail points. I open the little wooden garden gate. The now hot sun beats on my shoulders and will dry my blouse, in a while.

As I begin to weed, I lose where I am. There's Maman in her white cap and homespun dress. As she walks into her garden, she hums a French song, and she turns and looks at me. I know that it is she. And I know that she is alive. And my heart tries to break from my chest with joy. But only for a minute. Then, she's gone. Yet, that moment gives me strength.

Abigail hands me a little basket. "*Pour les framboises*", she says, pointing at the red berries: many hidden under leaves. I am happy to pick and maybe eat them. "Yes," I say in English, "I pick."

"Good words, Rose," she says, "You must learn English. The teacher will come soon."

The teacher? Oh, I remember. The teacher is Master Wells who helped me when I ran away from the village green. Later, he said to me in French, "We know of two little Acadian girls in a nearby village who are treated well. We'll try to be kind to you as well."

I go on picking and weeding and tidying the garden. The two little girls may be safe in that other village he called Southampton. But here, I am alone.

When Abigail calls me to eat, she first points at the well where I am to draw water. I draw up the bucket of water and then, although Jonas has not returned, we eat. The taste of this food is like a heavenly meal. It must be fish and onions and potatoes and herbs. I eat like a wolf.

After dinner Jonas returns and waves for me and Pegg to follow him into his wagon which he drives to a small green. On this grassy space are rough wooden pens filled with sheep racing to and fro. We hear shouts and see a cloud of dust blowing. Pegg reaches over to me and pats my arm. She tries to make me feel better, I know. And she does.

Jonas tries his horse at a hitching rack crowded with horses and wagons. He gives his mare water from a trough, turns and yells to us to get out of the wagon.

As we stand on the turf looking around, I turn to Pegg and make signs, "What is happening here?" But she puts her hands in the air and shakes her head. She can't explain.

Jonas points for us to wait as he wades into the flock of sheep, pushing them away until he picks one big-horned ram, grabs him by the neck, and throws him to the ground. He calls to us to hold the kicking terrified animal while Jonas looks at the animal's ear. I think there's a mark burned there that shows the sheep is Jonas's.

He calls us again to grab a thrashing animal's back legs and drag the ram to a table where other men are shearing their sheep. Jonas gets another man to help him lift the sheep onto the table and tie his legs. Master shears the fleece away from the ram's skin so that later, the sheep looks bare as a peeled apple.

Jonas makes us help other people in this task after we finished helping with his sheep. We work until my legs tremble; my shoulders ache and I am faint with tiredness...

Later, I am standing outside the pen with Pegg, waiting to see if Jonas calls us again when I hear, I think, "French girl!" spoken in French.

Spinning around, I see a tall, gawky, brown-haired girl, probably about my age, who looks very funny as her hair and her clothes are dotted with clumps of wool. It's so odd that I have to smile at her. She smiles back and speaks quickly and quietly in French. "You look funny too, your black hair has white spots of wool all over it."

I feel my mouth drop open and whisper, "What did you say?" in French.

Pegg grabs my arm. She points at the girl and says, "Sarah."

The girl smiles at me and says in poor French, "My father, teacher."

That I do understand. The teacher's the kind man who spoke French to me on the village green when we first came, and he said that he would try to help me.

I look up. But then Sarah vanishes in the crowd.

CHAPTER SEVENTEEN

ESCAPE

I keep looking around for this blond girl, Sarah. If she is the Teacher's daughter, she might be able to help me. But she is gone.

Finally, we climb back into the wagon with sheep's wool fleece stuffed all around us and Jonas turns back down the road to his house. Now I have free minutes, I look for Jacques everywhere. Please, Lord! He is small, and he needs me, please help me.

It's near dusk now. A bell rings and ahead I see a small boy moving cows from the village green down towards Jonas's house. It's a dark-haired boy and I look closely at him. It's not Jacques.

The boy opens Jonas's gate and Jonas's cow lumbers in, drops her head and begins to graze. Our wagon goes inside as well, and we climb down. Pegg goes to the barn and brings grain from the barn for the cow.

Jonas motions for me to carry some of the fleeces into a back part of the barn. I come out after the last one and Abigail calls from the garden, "Rose,"

"Yes," I nod, so tired.

"Milk the cow, Rose," Jonas says and points to the cow's shed.

It is near dark now, but I walk to the small shed. The cow lumbers in and I sit. Mistress has left a bucket and there is a bench in the corner. Stroking the cow's side, I pull gently on her teats until she relaxes and lets down her milk.

Losing myself in the familiar milking time, I'm in our old barn in Acadia, and then, suddenly, the cow bends her neck, looks around and kicks the bucket so that the milk spills.

"Aiyee!" I'm mad. Will Jonas punish me and call me stupid? His cow is stupid, not me, but I will be punished. I know it.

Leaving the bucket and the cow, I rush out of the yard and start running down a road that seems to go away from the village, but my legs soon give out and I cower in the pine shrubs.

It's not long before I hear the clip-clop of hooves and I slink back further into the piney woods. The horse and rider goes by and I see that it's Jonas. Throwing myself onto the soft moss, I hold my breath and try to rest. Later, the crackling of twigs alerts me that something is near me. The gentle noise stops.

Terrified, I lift my head. A native man is looking at me. I know he is native, for his skin is a rich brown and black hair falls from under his felt hat. He is not dressed in skins and feathers like the Mi'kmaq, he wears farmer's clothes.

He points to my moccasins, the ones Running Deer gave me in Acadia, and then to his own which are decorated with shells and pine needles like natives wear. There is a question in his eyes. But he never gets a chance to ask it.

Behind the native man stands Jonas. Jonas must have told the native to search me out and then, not seeing him, come back to look for him in the woods.

I get up and face Jonas, "I'm not your servant!" I tell him. But nothing changes. Jonas smiles his slow smile and hauls out a rope of vine and motions to the native man who must work for him, to tie my hands. I have to walk in front of them as Jonas pokes me in the back with his gun. When we get to the road, Jonas mounts his horse and tells the native man to lead me after him. We walk back to the large village green, where Jonas speaks to a man and the man points him towards the board with two holes in it mounted on a stake.

Quickly, I see what will happen next. I try to keep my voice calm, but it raises to a scream. I am so afraid.

"Do not speak French," he says and puts my hands in the holes and locks them there. I yell at him in French. He looks at me, smiles slowly and leaves.

It is dark. I am alone.

The whole night I sit trapped like a rat in a trap. My wrists chafe as I pull my hands back and forth through the rough holes in a board, to try to scratch at bug bites. My legs and privates smell from urine and body waste. There is no one about except one man who walks by with a lantern.

Several people leave their houses and walk past me. Black night descends and the damp chill licks my skin. I see no one, no star no moon. Flies bite me. My head drops down on the wooden board with a crack and I feel a bump rising on my forehead. I try to stay awake so that will not happen again.

In the early morning, boys toss balls at me. Finally, when the sun is high, a man comes and unlocks the board that holds me. But I can hardly stand, my joints are so cramped.

Stumbling towards Abigail and Jonas's house, I finally stand in front of the kitchen door. There is nowhere else to go. Will Jonas beat me if I return?

Finally, I raise my bleeding hands and knock.

CHAPTER EIGHTEEN

HELP

Abigail's mouth drops open as she turns from the fire and sees me. She waves me into the kitchen. "The little boys from the village told me just a few minutes ago," Abigail cries.

Jonas gets up without a word and walks out the door.

"Oh, Rose, what has he done?" she cries. "What has he done?"

She helps me sit on a bench, sends Pegg out to draw some well water and gently cleans my bleeding wrists, feet, and face. "He told me that he had found you and given you over to a village Clerk," Abigail says, "I thought that they might put you in the schoolhouse overnight to punish you, I had no idea he did this."

I don't understand all the things that she is saying. Her gentle hands wrapping my bleeding wrists tell me her sympathy.

I look at her and say, "Jacques?" For that is who I am worried about, not myself. "Is he still here?" I ask in French. "Has Master Jonas sent him away?"

"*Non*," she nods. "Soon, we go to see your little brother."

"*Oui*," I say, nodding my head vigorously.

"But we must put some chamomile paste on your wrists and wrap them, now," Abigail says and wraps my wrists carefully. They are so scratched and bleeding from trying to pull my hands out of the holes of the stocks. Then she wipes my face, especially my forehead, where I banged it and the bugs bit me. Her quiet care helps and I feel better. Lydia watches me like a little bird. I decide to play with her. My clucking like a hen makes Lydia laugh.

Mistress smiles as well and tells me in French to go out and gather eggs. I see a reed basket and make signs; Lydia and I will go to find eggs. But always, in my heart, I worry about Jacques, what will they do with him?

Before we leave, Abigail puts a hand on my arm, indicating that she wants me to wait. Her face is serious. Is it about Jacques?

"Jonas has gone to get the teacher," she says, "You must learn English."

"No!" I snap back quickly, thinking of the English forcing us onto ships.

"Yes," Abigail says softly. "You must. People here hate the French. They will hate you if you speak French."

"Why so angry against French?" I ask.

"French army kill sons of this village."

"Mama," Little Phoebe chirps from her dolly corner, "my doll is hungry."

Abigail turns to her bright-eyed, red-haired daughter, "Well, we just will have to give him some samp, yes?"

She puts a tiny bowl in front of the doll, sees that the girls are busy. Then Mistress turns to me, "I've heard that all Acadians captured by the English must give up their papist religion."

I shake my head. I have no words to say how cruel this is.

Jonas throws open the house door with a bang. Shakily, I stand. Behind him stands the tall, slim, bearded Teacher, who spoke to me in French: when I ran away from the crowd on the village green.

Jonas steps into the kitchen. Behind him is the man and then, the girl I think is named Sarah, the girl I saw at the sheep shearing.

The man greets Mistress Abigail. He speaks to her pointing to his mouth and my ear and shaking his head. I guess that he asks if he can speak in French.

Then he says to me in French, "My daughter Sarah will teach you English." He smiles fondly at his daughter.

I shake my head, "*Non!*"

Master Jonas bursts out with angry words and points at me. "English, yes!" he says.

Mistress Abigail holds her hand up as if to protect herself, and me, from his anger. She points to a bucket for me to leave the room and draw water from the pump for the garden.

Sarah walks beside me and helps me carry the big bucket and as we walk to the garden, she whispers in French, "It's right, Rose, I'll help you."

Surprised by her kindness, I gather myself together to ask her in the lowest voice that I can, "Jacques, where is he?"

Sarah grunts rudely and seems to ignore me, "Come with me," she commands in a rough voice. I notice then that Jonas stands nearby.

We take the filled water bucket to the garden and water the dye plants. Then, Sarah grabs my hand and pulls me back towards the Bellows' house. "Come," she says roughly, again. We go into the kitchen with the bucket. Abigail points us to a pile of sheep wool fleeces.

Sarah says roughly to me, "Pick them up." When I fill my arms, my face is nearly in the pile. I choke as I follow Sarah out to her Papa's wagon.

As we get closer to the wagon, Sarah points to where I should put the wool in the back beside a load of firewood and then, out of earshot of Jonas, she whispers in French in my ear. "Your little brother, Jacques, lives close by."

My heart leaps. "Can we see him?" I ask quickly.

"No, it's too soon. Master Jonas might get angry," she says. "I will try to find out more and tell you when you come to my home."

I lift my eyes again to her sea-blue eyes and smile.

Sarah squeezes my hand, hops up into the wagon, her father comes and grabs the reins and their horse clip-clops down to the gate to the road.

I am so happy that I learn of Jacques.

At dusk, I get a bowl of mush in the corner. At home, I might have had cabbage and pork. Oh, how I would love to have a piece of fried pork. At least, Abigail has sprinkled a few berries on my samp, which I've learned is what the mush is called. But I am still hungry. I wish that I could eat a chicken fricot from my sturdy Acadian cook pot.

CHAPTER NINETEEN

FORT OSWEGO

The next day. In the misty, damp weather, laundry will not dry, so we do not wash. I'm glad as my hands are scratched from my run in the piney woods and my time in the stocks and I twisted my ankles as well. Abigail seems to pity me as she gives me a little extra food.

"Today, we will see your little brother," she says to me suddenly.

"Oh!" I choke on my piece of morning bread.

"He stays with Nate and his family, and I told Jonas this morning that I will go to ask Nate, as he is good with fixing things, to fix our butter churn. It has sprung a leak."

"Oh! "I can hardly speak. I'm so surprised, "*Bien*."

As we walk down the road, Lydia and Phoebe skip along beside us. I stroll along happy to be out of the house and away from Master. We see a group of women walking along together...

When they get closer, the women call out a pleasant greeting to Abigail. One woman, smiling, calls, "Miller Samuel is slow grinding today."

But they look at me with a sour expression. One young woman speaks to Abigail. I hear a few words and see her look at me. "Is she French?" the girl asks.

"She is not French," answers Abigail curtly. "She is Rose the Acadian."

A low murmur of grumbles hangs in the air and some of the women turn away from me. Abigail ignores the ill-speaking women.

I cannot speak to them. I cannot even look at them. But inside, I try to be strong.

Very soon, Abigail stops in front of a fence with a gate. Behind the fence is a plain house with several sheds and wagons about it. She calls, "Nate!"

After a short time, a young man with a shy smile on his face walks out to the gate. I notice his blue eyes. He glances at me and looks respectfully at Abigail.

"Can I help, Mistress Abigail?" he asks.

"Can you fix my butter churn, Nate? Ours has a crack in it." Abigail's voice is warm. She must like this big, strong, good-natured fellow. And I can see why. His manner is winning. His smile is easy and relaxed.

"Papa says that I am doing fair work now," he says in a confident voice. "I will come this afternoon to fix it."

He, I sense, is a little like André in his gentle yet confident manner. Of course, André, if he is still alive, is dark haired and slim.

Nate turns to me unexpectedly. "Jacques here," he says, looking at me kindly.

"Where is he?" I burst out. I speak French but Nate must know that I want to see my brother.

"James!" Nathaniel calls loudly.

Jacques runs out from a shed. He sees me. "Rose!" Jacques flings himself upon me. I feel his ribs, he is so skinny. But I also feel the strength in his arms. I hug him very tightly. Then, I stoop down and hold him away and look. His brown eyes hold the spark of merriness that he always had before. Skinny, yes, but cheery as he often was at home.

In French, he says to me, "Where is Pierre?"

I shake my head, and he starts to cry. "I want Pierre."

Nate grips his shoulder and says something in English, pointing to a small barn beside the house. "Go," he tells Jacques.

Jacques sniffles and chokes but wipes his tears and runs over to the little barn. When he comes back, he shows me a chair leg that he cut out with a small chisel from a prepared block.

"*Bien*?" He asks Nate in his clear piping voice.

"Good," Nathaniel says firmly. "Say words in English."

"Good," Jacques repeats in a whisper.

Nathaniel shyly looks me in the face. "Mistress?" He asks.

"Rose," I say.

"James good boy," he says slowly, pointing at my brother. "But may go," he waves his hand as if he says goodbye."

"NO!" I burst out, but Nate has gone back to his house.

"Rose, we must hurry home now," Mistress says. She turns quickly, pulls at the little girls' hands and starts off at a fast pace for her home. I turn to follow her but Jacques rushes after me, holding onto my skirt and trying to stop me.

I clutch him tightly. But Nate comes back out and gently pulls my brother away from me. "Like boy," he says, "But Papa," he waves his hand goodbye.

Nate picks Jacques up like a struggling puppy and goes inside the shed.

Abigail calls back to me, "Hurry," she says, "Master Jonas will be angry if we are not there to boil up a chicken for dinner. Hurry!" She adds curtly.

I hear Jacques screaming but I walk quickly after Abigail. It is terrible to leave him.

As I walk behind her, "Rose, will you hurry?" Abigail calls again.

I call Abigail and try to walk faster to catch up with her. I know that I can help her cook, so she will not be late with the meal if she will let me.

Soon we are at her garden gate. Jonas, hoeing in the garden, stands up and looks with a sour expression at Abigail. "I thought the French girl was to weed the garden," he says, "This a mess of weeds."

Abigail's face sinks thin with fatigue. Her shoulders droop, and she drops her head. "I thought that I told you to do that, Rose," she lies.

"I did not have time to finish," I say. I grip my little bird, *Espère*, in my pocket before I say quietly, "But I can help you with dinner."

Abigail barely nods, so I quickly go out to the garden where she has her herbs and grab a handful of basil and some chives. When I come in, I pick up the chicken and make motions to cut it into pieces, she nods yes and smiles and sinks on a bench.

I pull out my fricot pan and *saute* the chicken and herbs until the chicken is done. I know where the milk and butter are and the buckwheat flour, and soon have a nice dish of chicken cooking in a sauce. We send the girls out for some early greens. After Jonas returns, and he and Abigail have eaten with spoons, the girls and I stand around the table and eat with our fingers. Pegg finishes the dish.

Later, as I wearily turn towards the garden to weed, I hear men's voices in the parlor.

The men in the parlor argue. One voice speaks out clearly and a hush falls on the others. The clear voice may be Master Wells, the schoolmaster. The voice is loud. I think he is reading something to the others. I've seen here that people read from sheets of paper with words printed on them... *Le Journal*, I think they call those pages.

I hear a few French words: names of forts that were in or near Acadia. I know the words Fort Beauséjour and Fort Louisburg. I think that I hear Fort Oswego, but that name I don't know.

The men who listen stamp their feet and raise their voices when they hear the words, "Fort Oswego." The men's voices rise like a wild wind and they spit out words angrily. I guess that they are upset over a French victory over their English soldiers. One man, while walking through the kitchen, spits at me. With a dark look, he opens the kitchen door and leaves. I scramble up the ladder to the loft.

Through the floorboards, later, I can see and hear Jonas and Abigail in the kitchen. The men have left.

She holds up the news; sheets and reads to him. Jonas walks up and down with a heavy step, spinning around quickly as he turns. His voice sounds sharp and bitter. I hear Abigail say something about "The French and Oswego." Her voice trembles.

Jonas bursts out and says something about I think I hear Ephraim.

Abigail shakes her head. I see Abigail's hand shaking as well.

Jonas stares at her and shakes his head and points towards the attic where I sleep with Pegg. Then he walks with a heavy step to the stairs and goes up to their bedroom.

Wearily, with her huge stomach in her way, Abigail walks to the fire and I can hear her poking it with a stick to break up the embers so the fire will damp for the night. Phoebe calls out in her sleep from the bed that the two little girls share off the kitchen. Abigail calls to her softly.

After this day, I begin to know that the sour looks people give me are not for me; they are for the enemy French. The French Army has killed boys from this village.

CHAPTER TWENTY

NEW PATHWAYS

Pegg has been watching me from her corner of the attic. I can tell from her face that she wonders what is happening below the stairs. I shake my head at her and smile a little.

Like a kitten, I scramble to my thin pallet, twist around and try to sleep. I pray. "Help me, God, to be together with my loved ones; Maman, Madeleine, Jacques, Pierre, Mary Josèphe and André: wherever they are."

It seems so long ago that I lived in Acadia and told Papa that I wanted to be a strong Acadian woman. Papa is looking down on me now from heaven. I will go on. It is hard for me to know why Jonas is mean to me. That is harder. But I'll be strong and speak out and not let him destroy my spirit and faith.

On Sunday, Abigail insists that I go to church with her and the children although Jonas does not go. Inside the church, I am not allowed to sit with them, I must sit with the slaves and the servants. At the second sermon that the Minister named Buell gives, I fall asleep. It is by now three o'clock in the afternoon. Church bell tolls the hours above us. I understand nothing of the first two-hour sermon.

My head falls with a hard clunk on the board in front of the servants' space. Everyone turns to look at me. A man comes up behind me and pokes my back with a sharp stick.

A few people stare at me with an accusing look on their faces, and that makes me angry.

Oh, how I miss *Église St-Jean-Baptiste*, the little Catholic church in Annapolis Royal. All the Acadians and Native peoples sang in French, and the feeling of the love of the Lord filled my heart.

I have no idea if Catholic priests even exist in America. How strange. I thought before that the Lord created one church and that was the Catholic church. But now, these people think the same thing about their church. The church name is hard to hear, I think it starts, "Presby" but cannot understand the rest.

When we finally leave the church, Nate has brought Jacques and I can talk to my dear little brother away from the others for a few minutes. And then, there, thank God, is my new friend, Sarah.

Sarah tells me her last name is Wells. She whispers to me in French and says that I have been given leave to go with her, soon to visit her house. It seems that Abigail talked Jonas into letting me go, so that I can learn learn English from her father, the teacher, Master Wells. "And" Sarah adds with a secretive smile, "we can have fun as well!"

I smile, nod, and say, "*Oui*." But, I add, firmly, "No want to speak English."

It is good to be with the Wells who understand that although I speak French, I am not a French person like the people the East Hampton men fight against, that I'm an Acadian.

My ancestors came from France, but the people I am part of live in a place in Canada called Acadia, and we think of that as our country, for we have lived there for about one hundred and fifty years.

Next day, after I finish my chores, I hear a steady clip-clop stop at our gate. It's Sarah in her wagon. Abigail sees her as well and cries out a greeting. She waves for me to go with Sarah, so I climb into the wagon and soon we are traveling along dirt roads.

"How feel you this afternoon, Rose?" Sarah asks.

I shrug my shoulder and turn away from her. Even sitting beside Sarah in the wagon as I am now, my thoughts are too mixed up to talk about.

Sarah turns from driving the horse and looks at me. "I'm sorry, Rose. I cannot know how hard it is for you." She is quiet for a moment. "But I hope that soon you will have something to feel good about," she says quietly, "Well, like having me as a friend," she adds, with a smile on her face.

I smile and say, "Yes, that is good! It's the best... but so much is... *c'est terrible*." My voice trails off like I have run out of ideas, but... that is not true. "Life here is hard. I can work hard. But to live, hated by people... I feel lost. I want to be with my own family and friends."

Sarah looks over at me and I see the care in her blue eyes.

"*Oui*," she says. We both hear the clip-clop of the old horse and feel the sun.

And I retreat again into my thought.

We pass a cherry tree that lies close to the road. Sarah turns to me, and points to the cherries. "Would you like some?" she asks. I nod and she pulls the horse to a stop, hands me the reins and jumps down. She lightly leaps the mud puddles, goes into the trees and carefully picks and fills her apron with fruit. Taking off her apron, she ties it in a bundle and climbs back up to the wagon seat.

I nibble at them. "*Bonnes*," I sigh. The breeze and the sun touch my cheeks. Fishing boats sail into the harbor off to our right, salt in the breeze fills my nose.

We turn down a lane towards the water. Ahead of us, in the rippling waves, children prowl in the mudflats. Every once in a while, one stops, squats down and digs in the muck with a stick.

"Sarah, what do they do?" I ask.

Sarah drops the reins and makes a motion of opening a shell. She says, "Clams!"

"Clams," I say. I smack my lips and lift my hand as with a spoon for soup.

"Yes," Sarah says and then "A new English word, yes?"

"Yes, clams," I repeat.

The horse has stopped. Sarah yanks at the reins to get the old horse's head out of the grass. The wagon comes out of the shade of the trees. High above, birds ride the wind currents over the water. Their rough shrieks pierce my ears. The horse trots into a yard and stops with a jolt that brings the wagon up to her tail.

The wagon stands in front of a sagging, grey shingled cottage. Yards away, water laps the beach. Sarah jumps down as a little boy races out the cottage door. "Wait, Jonathan," she says to him as he hangs on her skirt. "If you let go, I will let you take the mare to pasture."

The wagon creaks as I jump down too. I rub the mare's head between her eyes as she turns patiently to look at us. We untie the traces from the collar to the wagon. And I think of Plume, our horse in Acadia. He was so beautiful, so spirited, not like this old mare.

We rub the mare's back a little to ease her muscles, and when we finish, Sarah calls, "Here you are!" to Jonathan. A big smile lights Jonathan's face. He takes the lead line that Sarah hands to him and the old mare ambles behind him down a rocky path to the meadow.

Already, I feel comfortable here and yet I do not know why I find it so. Perhaps because I can laugh with Sarah. Perhaps because it is less neat and orderly here than in the fenced yards of East Hampton village. One breathes more freely, it seems.

Near me, a huge anchor leans crazily against a shack. Fishing nets sprawl on the meadow fence and a rowboat lies on the beach above the seaweed line.

Sarah steps up close to me and whispers in my ear. "Maman may be a bit angry. She and Papa wanted me to hurry here, so that we could have lots of time for lessons. I thought of that when we got the cherries, but then I forgot." She pounds her head with one hand, grins and says, "Come quickly now!"

Side by side we walk towards the house. It is not trim or square, like most of the homes in East Hampton village. This house rambles like a stream finding its bed. The front part has two windows poking through the roof and the back part is on one floor and encloses a garden. The house is low-roofed, and swallows dart in and out of the eaves.

I clutch my little carved swallow, *Espère*, trapped in my cloth pocket. I think how dark and hot it is in my pocket. Like my little swallow, I want to swoop and dive and be free to move about as I wish. Will I ever be free? Ever?

A woman with a long face and wisps of blond hair peeking out from her cap stands at the door, "Come in, daughter. You are late," she says. That much I can understand.

"Yes, Maman," Sarah says, leaning across the half-door to peck her cheek with a kiss. "Don't be angry."

"Oh, Sarah," her mother smiles and then a frown wrinkles her forehead, "Be quick, now."

CHAPTER TWENTY-ONE

LEARNING THE TRUTH

"Rose," Mistress Well says. She puts her hands on my shoulders and looks into my eyes, "Sarah told me about you. Welcome!"

I feel the warmth of her greeting, smile at her, and bob my head as I would have done to my aunties or bonne grand-mère at home. Looking around, my eyes adjust to the darkness inside the house. Spinning wheels, a small loom, rough chairs, and a table take shape out of the gloom. Light enters only through a row of windows at the harbor side of the room.

Just as my eyes get used to the dark, Sarah shows me where to hang my cloak behind the door. "Come, Rose," she says and pushes my elbow, so I turn, and then I hear a baby's soft cry.

Close to the harbor windows, I see Sarah's mother cuddling a baby. Golden afternoon light falls on her and the baby nuzzling for a breast. I hear the baby cry softly again and then she nurses.

There they are, Sarah's mother and her sweet child...
and where are my mother, and my little sister, Madeleine?
My throat chokes and I have to wipe my eyes.

Looking up I see Sarah's father sitting at a table
strewn with a trencher, a bowl of yellow and green squash
and a book. Master Wells pushes his chair back with a
screeching sound and gets up from the table.

"Welcome, Rose," he says in French. "You are late,
so I will teach you myself. We have work to do. Are you
ready?"

He is very tall, I realize. He steps towards me and a
smile flits across his trim bearded face. Speaking French,
he says, "It will not be easy for you, Rose. But I do want
to help you. If you can learn English, the town folk will
think kindly of you."

"*Non, Maître*," shaking my head violently I resist.

"Rose," he says in French. "you have no choice.
Please try, it will help you."

"Master, it will be hard for me," I say softly in
English, encouraged by his kind manner. "I have to work
so hard. My head is so tired."

"You will do it," he says in a firm teacher's voice.
"We do not have much time; the afternoon moves on. Let
us begin! Come to the table here." Master looks at me. I

sense that he sees into my thoughts. "Before you leave today, I will speak to you again about, other matters," he says. "Now, begin! Sit here." He points to the table and removes the vegetables and the trencher, creating a clear space for work.

"Sarah, help your mother with the baby. I will teach Rose now," he says.

I sit, and Master stands up. He is a teacher now, not a papa. Nervously, I listen to him and strain my ears to hear the correct way to say the English words he speaks. Sometimes, he explains meanings in French words first, "Jonas is a weaver, as well as a farmer," he says in French. "It will be helpful for you to know the names of some of the plants that he uses. He may want you later to help Abigail make different color dyes, from the plants.

The light from the window dims, but Master does not stop. I learn simple words because he is so sure that I will learn. "Can I help you?" "a bucket of water," "weed the garden," he speaks the words in French first and then in English and explains their meaning.

Finally, Master says, "Rose, you have done well. You must come again next Sunday." I stand respectfully, bow, and turn from the table.

Sarah's maman cuts me a hunk of bread. I sling my patched cloak over my shoulder with one hand and gnaw the bread with the other. I am always hungry and am nearly finished when Master walks over to me. He speaks in French now. "There are things you should know now," he says. "Wait a bit before you leave."

"Yes, Master Wells," I say, with my heart trembling, full of both fear and yes, hope.

"Sarah, go and harness the horse, and be ready to leave. I must have words with our young friend." Master puts a hand on my arm, "come, let us talk."

"Rose, you did not have much time this afternoon so now I will speak quickly in French, so that you understand what I will tell you."

He asks, "Is it hard to be with the Bellows?"

I nod. "Yes, Master," I say, "Master Jonas is very difficult, *difficile*.'

"He is difficult. I know that. You are there for the sake of his wife, Abigail. I know her well and worry about her."

"Ah?" I ask, surprised.

"Jonas lost his first wife to smallpox. Recently he got word that he lost his son, to the bullets of the French. He is very sad at heart and angry at everyone... not only you. He connects you somehow to the loss of his son, Ephraim, and feels that you bear a share in that tragedy because he thinks of you as French."

All these words swirl around in my head. I clutch *Espère* but still cannot forgive Jonas for his actions against me. "And Mistress Abigail?" I ask.

"He's angry at her, too. Abigail is the daughter of my friend, a schoolteacher in New Haven. Abigail came here with me to help in the schoolroom and later, she met Jonas. Eventually, he asked her to marry him. But it has not worked out well."

A breath of fresh air swept through my head. Poor Abigail. That explains why she is so kind to me when Jonas is away… and why she knows French. But when he is home, I see that she fears him. She does not protect me from him. Now that I know why, I am a little sorry for her.

But I must take care of myself. I will not depend on her.

"*Je comprends*," I say, as all these words sink in: feeling that I am in a pool of light that circles just the two of us, that there is no-one else in this world except Master and me. He goes on.

"It is a hard life you have come upon, Rose. But all is not lost. Work hard with these lessons in English. They will help you. I will watch out for you in the Bellows home as much as I can."

I just look at him, for a moment, letting his words sink into my spirit.

"*Merci Bien* Master," I whisper.

"Yes!" he says and stands at his full height. "But It is too early yet to plan your escape from here. You have Marie Josèphe and Jacques to think of, as well as yourself. It is very difficult... But we will try. We will talk again," he says.

"But, when?" I beg.

"Patience, child," he says softly.

The look on Master's face closes down like a shut door. I cannot ask questions he does not want to answer, so I walk shakily over to the door. Sarah's mother hugs me warmly. Jonathan holds the hitched mare until Sarah, and I get into the wagon.

I know that I must get home to Jonas's, to do the farm chores and help Abigail's children. The mare reluctantly trots as she reaches the road. We turn left towards East Hampton.

The help and comfort I felt at Sarah's house stays with me as a glow inside my spirit, like an afternoon in my old village in Acadia when all seemed right as I walked home along the river and saw the ducks settle into the marshes for the night… when I knew my home was up the road and felt loved and protected.

I am on my own now. But here, I have found friends.

I hang on to the wagon seat as we bang our way back to Jonas's house. A neat cluster of grey houses flows by us. Candles flicker through their windows as dusk falls. Dread of Jonas sweeps over me. But I brush it off. Whatever lies ahead this quiet evening, I can do… Soon, I find myself in front of the Bellow's house. It is, suddenly, the moment when darkness falls.

"Take care, Rose," Sarah says in a low voice as I climb down from the wagon. I cannot see her face.

"I will, Sarah," I say clearly in English.

Jonas stands outside the house. He does not look happy. "Abigail has fallen sick," he growls. "Get to work. Help her, bank the fire, feed the children, get my supper, put the children to bed…" Could he not do some of these tasks himself? He stops spouting and at least turns to the barn to milk the cow.

I practically throw myself down from the wagon. Confidently I call, "Yes, Master," open the gate, and walk up the path. I hear the footfalls of Sarah's horse fade away. I open the house door.

CHAPTER TWENTY-TWO

HEART TO HEART

Mistress Abigail must feel sickly as Pegg stirs the pot over the embers and serves up a bowl for each of the girls.

"Some food, Pegg?" I ask.

"Yes, um Rose." We look at each other. She gives me some soup, and I feel very close to her…

The girls finish their soup and go to their tiny room off the kitchen.

I sit for a moment by the fire, reflecting on all this: Abigail heavy with child, the girls sometimes running wild, and suddenly I, who hated coming to this place and this family, feel real worry about the girls and Abigail. My life is mixed up with theirs. Yet, I still have my dream of freedom. I will never lose that!

The noise of scraping chairs and men's voices startles me. Jonas and the gentlemen in the front room pass me on the way out. I think that I hear the word "Acadian" spoken by one man. Another one says something to his friend about "Acadians and battayes," He looks at me and shakes his head as he goes by. "French aliens," he spits the words out towards me. Jonas opens and closes the kitchen door and goes out with the others.

I wonder why those men were here? Did I truly hear the word Acadian? I've been so upset about Jacques that I have no idea why the men met.

I go to hear the girls' prayers. Soon, they are fast asleep in their little beds. Let them rest. I raise my hand and bless them quietly. Now that Jonas has gone out, I can see Abigail for a moment. I have to see how sick she is, is it the coming birth, or is it worse like bad breathing or pains in her chest that kept her in bed?

In the front of the house, a stairway leads up to Jonas and Abigail's bedroom. Quietly, I climb the stairs and tiptoe into the room. It is dark, except for a candle on a stand on the far side of the curtained bed. I tiptoe over the rag rug and stand at the near side of the bed. Abigail opens her eyes.

"Hello, Rose," she says sleepily.

"Pegg told me that you were sickly tonight, Mistress. Master Jonas has gone out. I came to see how you were feeling." I speak in French,

Abigail's eyes light on me, and she shakes her head. "I have to get my brain to work in French, Rose," she says. "I was sleeping."

She smiles weakly. I watch her for a moment and see that she is trying to get her French into her brain. "How was the English lesson, Rose? Did you learn a lot?" she finally says in French.

I smile, "I did learn… a little."

"Tonight, we'll speak French. I think I can manage," Abigail says. And my heart warms by her kindness.

"*Merci*, Mistress." I look at her and bob my head. She looks so tired now. She's lost weight, probably because she can't keep much down in her stomach. Her skin is drawn into wrinkles around her mouth and across her brow. Her lovely green eyes are dull.

"How are you, this moment?" I say very quietly, "Are you feeling a little better? Does the baby move?"

"Today, I was so sick," Abigail says. "But tonight, I feel better though weak. And yes the baby kicks, hard!" She closes her eyes again.

I quietly sit on the side of the bed.

"Do stay for a while, Rose," she says. "I worry now that the baby might come when I am alone."

I continue to sit. The candle on the stand flickers and sputters. I think of the girls and decide it will worry Abigail to tell her of their adventure out to the barn with a candle last night and say nothing about it.

Abigail closes her eyes and breathes deeply as if she is in a deep sleep. But then she speaks again and clears her throat nervously. "Rose?"

"Yes, Mistress."

"Rose, you have come to us in a sad way. I am sorry for you. But I'm glad that you're here."

I cannot say the same words to her. It is not in my heart to say that I am glad that I am here. It is too difficult for me. So, I just say, "Yes, Mistress," and continue to sit quietly.

"Rose, I know so little about you. Your home, your parents, your loves…"

As I hear these words, I remember my shock that night in my home when André came, when he asked me to leave Acadia with him. A tear slides down my cheek. In the half-darkness, I lose my control and sob.

Her quiet voice asks in French. "Rose, you left someone in Acadia?"

"I left no one there. We were all put on ships. But, yes, there was someone... I felt so young, I was not ready to marry him then. And in the Great Leaving, he was put on another ship from mine."

I speak slowly in French, so that she can understand. I wipe my eyes and clear my throat. "Later, and in recent days, I do think of him. His name was André. He loved me." I cannot go on, turn away and sit quietly.

"I am sorry, Rose," Abigail finally says. "I do not need to know more, if it makes you sad to think about it."

"Master Jonas will be home soon, Mistress. Call me if you need me," I say. I stand for a moment by her head and look at her already closing eyes.

Quietly, I steal out of the room and down the stairs. I give the fire a poke and put on a small log to keep it burning through the night. Then, I climb the ladder to the cold attic.

Pegg's regular breathing comes from the spot closest to the brick chimney. I use the chamber pot awkwardly. Then I climb under my blanket. The sky through the window is deep black. The stars seem very close. So as to not think about Jacques and that he might be sent away from me, I think back on the visit I have just had: a closer touch of hearts than Abigail and I have had before.

I am thankful for Mistress Abigail's kindness to me. But still, I am only a step above a slave here. I can never be happy here. Pegg will never be happy here. Our lives, our people are not here. We have been forced to live here.

And yet, and yet, now I know what Teacher Wells told me, that Abigail is from off-Long Island and not well-liked. When Abigail is weak from childbirth, and sick, who will help her? The women in the village may be afraid of Jonas's bad temper. They may not help her as they would another new mother. She is not of them. She is from off-island.

My heart is torn, thinking of Abigail with a tiny baby, alone with Jonas and I try to resolve that for now, I will help the Mistress as much as I can.

"Love your neighbor as yourself," the old priest in Acadia used to preach: that's what Acadians do.

Finally, my eyes droop. We will see what tomorrow holds. Perhaps there will be more talk of Acadians. Perhaps Abigail's baby will be born... and there will be joy, and yet more work. I twist myself into the blanket. If only I could speak with Marie Josèphe! ...we could try to plan our escape to freedom.

CHAPTER TWENTY-THREE

FREE ACADIANS

"Come girls, we will sweep the house just like Maman likes it. And if you do a good job, we may go for a walk to the beach in the late afternoon," I say the next day. It is a warm sunny day in early summer.

Pegg straightens her apron and her cap. "I'll do the milking. Girls do you want to come?" she asks. After they finish sweeping, the girls trail after her out the door.

I leave the top half of the door open. The sun has a glow that touches things with gold. I feel touched by a glint of the golden light, hope springs in my heart after my visit with Sarah and her family.

I hear the girls talking in the garden. Pegg must have set them to weed the bean rows. I heat up a stewed meat dish and freshen it with green chives and thyme and set it to simmer for our mid-day meal.

When the girls come in, they take a small bowl upstairs to Abigail and then call Pegg to eat. After the girls work carding wool, I tell them, happily, "To the beach!"

We take a wandering walk from the North Village towards the sea, the ocean sweeps softly onto the sand today. I leave my shawl in the beach grass and walk barefoot in the water, warmed by the late afternoon sun. The girls take their baskets, and each looks for shells. Phoebe dumps any little piece of shell in, but Lydia looks carefully for whole shells. She does not take the common scallops but looks for whole whelks and new kinds of shells.

My spirit feels free on the beach. I remember when I was the girls' age. I searched the banks of La Rivière Dauphin for pretty rocks. Now, the ocean breeze, the golden light, a search for shells is enough. Keeping an eye on the children, I roam the dunes.

I look up frequently for Lydia might decide to walk in the shallows, and people tell me that the currents pull fast down the beach, here. I look up again.

There I see five or six large canoës in the ocean, coming from the west. I rub my eyes. The boats have small sails. A few are paddled only. Soon, they are a few hundred yards out from where we are on the beach. I see five of them, and as they get closer, seeing us, they angle into the shore. I am stunned by sight and run to take the girls away from the surf line. We stand up by the seagrass, ready to run, as the boats crash over gravel and broken shells onto the beach. A nearly naked big, strong man sees me. He waves his arm and shouts.

"*Nous sommes acadiens*. We are Acadians," he says. Impossible! But his accent is authentic. I know that speech. How can they be here? From where did they come? Have they dropped out of the sky?

"*Oui*!" I cry. As Lydia and Phoebe hang back in the beach grass, I go back down on the beach. I cry, "*Je suis acadienne!*"

Weak cheers, and cries of joy, from these people. They climb from the boats and stumble towards me. The girls whimper in their hiding place.

These people are mostly naked with wild hair and beards. Standing a hundred yards from them, I call in French, "Who are you? Where are you from?"

A young woman answers that they are Acadians who were sent from Acadia to South Carolina. They got permission to leave South Carolina and sail back to wherever they could find Acadia. She says that, for weeks, in hot sun and storms, they have followed the coastline of America. They stopped at beaches on the way and begged for food or caught fish to eat.

An old woman walks closer. I see sores oozing on her face. Her cracked lips bleed. She calls that they have no idea where they are. But they desire to go back to Acadia. For that they have paddled for hundreds of miles. She asks me how far it is to Acadia?

Other ragged people call out. They smile an unbelieving smile when they hear me speak Acadian French. One old man calls excitedly to his son, "Is this Acadia. Have we reached our beloved land again?"

My heart sinks, I tell them, I say in French, "I have not a good idea of where Acadia is, from here. I think that it is North. But it must be very far away. Big ships brought us here from Acadia. Ships that sailed days through the ocean."

As I look at them, I know that I am one of them and I want to go with them. I could climb into that boat and sail away. We would float to who knows where. How would that be? I could be free, free of the bitter Jonas, free of English ways! I myself could choose to do that, and I would be free.

But I would leave my little brother and Marie Josèphe, and Pierre, who is somewhere. I would abandon these two little girls on a deserted beach, with the tide rising.

I can't do it. Tears stream down my cheeks. I stand speechless, looking at these hardly human people, they are so bony. and ragged. But they are my people. And they are free! These ragged people are my people. I drop my head and choke back sobs.

One of the elders asks for food and drink.

For that, I have to lead them back to the village. They look too weak to continue and where else would I send them? But I am afraid, for them. Speaking in French, I tell them to pull up their canoes and come with me.

They pull up their boats above the waterline. There are about fifty people. Jonas's little girls look at their ragged clothes and wild hair and run out of the beach grass to hold my hands. One of the women speaks a little English and speaks kindly to the girls.

The girls are afraid of these strange people that have just arrived from the ocean. But they hold my hands tight and Phoebe chatters, "Will you take them to my Papa?" Lydia asks, "Can we help them and give them food?"

"We will see," is all I dare say. We straggle along over the dunes and the beach road, ambling as they are so weak, until we come to Jonas's house. His horse is tied to the rack.

As villagers see us and hear about them, they run out of their houses and surround the Acadians. I remember with fear what that felt like and try to make hand signals to the villagers to stand back. I try to speak, "Please stand back!" I say to the villagers. I see one of Nate's helpers, a man I know understands my French and call him by name. He stands by me as I speak and translates to tell the villagers who these people are.

"These people are Acadians like me. They were given leave to find their way back to Acadia. They came in on boats to the ocean beach."

The crowd at first mutters and looks darkly at these ragged folk. Jonas hears them and comes out. I look to Jonas for guidance. Brusquely, he tells me to have these people sit down on the grass, now. One of the younger Acadian men speaks kindly to Lydia.

"Silence!" Jonas orders. The town trustees come. I am told to speak to the Acadians and try to interpret as well as I can, what the Acadian leader says. I re-tell in English as well as I can: a sad story of two months scudding the sea from South Carolina. I say though, that these Acadian people were free to leave that colony and seek their fortune.

As I help to encourage talk between the new Acadian people and the town people, I talk to a young Acadian man in French. He tells me that he came from near my village, that he and the others were loaded on a ship at the same time that we were, stuffed into cargo space and sailed for weeks on end to South Carolina. And in answer to my questions about my family he says he saw Maman put onto the schooner *Dove* with André, his mother and Madeleine.

Oh my G…! My heart leaps!

Is she still alive? Or did she die like Papa, and where are little Madeleine and André? The young man has no idea. His brown eyes catch mine with kindness.

The English know where the The *Dove* was sent to land passengers. But I don't. I must find them. I must!

Some villagers have gone back to their homes to bring bread and water to these ragged travelers. Most of the Acadians smile their thanks and gulp the food in a minute.

As all of this goes on in my head and in front of me, I hear the sound of drums coming up the village road from the Town Hall. Our heads turn and we see a small group of ragged colonial militia. They carry guns. They march towards the ragged Acadians.

I hold my breath. Please, please do not harm them, don't stop these Acadians.

And then the town crier calls out. A kindly villager translates his words to me. "This group of French aliens was seen from shore several times as they followed the coastline of Long Island. Word was sent from Governor Hardy of New York to the commandant of British forces in Brooklyn. The troops have been on their trail for days. These are the orders the Governor gave. "These Acadians are to be captured and put into indentured service in New York City."

Rage rises in my throat. I look away, look away from these poor souls. I shake inwardly. This is not right. They are free, from South Carolina.

And if this can happen to them, it might happen to us. I see some faces of our East Hampton villagers that are touched with pity, but not all of them Guns are raised. The militia moves in on them. Weak yells rise from the poor battered Acadians.

I am told to tell them their fate. I have to call out loudly in French, for they see that they are trapped and are crying and screaming for freedom. I try to start again. Tears stream down my face; I tell them the cruel news. One woman rushes up to me and pulls my hand with her hand; so bony that it hurts.

"No! We will die before this. We have our freedom!" she screams. "Have mercy!"

The militia men take her away. All the Acadians are forced to move, under guard, up the hill to behind the meeting house.

Lydia's clear voice rings out, "Rose, help them!"

All around us the villagers murmur and most say, "They were free. This cannot be."

But Jonas says, "do not protest Rose, or you may go with them," or something like that. I stop listening.

I cannot help them. No one here can. These soldiers are under the orders of Governor Hardy. I tell Lydia and Phoebe this. I whisper in their ears, "It is not right."

We all slowly go to our homes. No one speaks. When we reach home, Pegg does not understand but she puts hot bacon and cabbage in the trenchers for our dinner meal. And that makes it worse, for unknown to her such food is Acadian fare and I think again of my dear family.

In the morning, Pegg tells me, the Acadians are gone!

But my search for Maman and André and Madeleine begins.

CHAPTER TWENTY-FOUR

DISCOVERY

The next morning when I walk out in the yard to get some water, my legs feel cold under my petticoat and skirt. "Brr, *il fait froid ce matin*," I say to myself… and think of the Acadians perhaps loaded onto a ship from Sag Harbor for the voyage to New York City, with practically no clothes on their backs, getting soaked, going through the rough waves of Hell-Gate.

"Who are you talking to?" A pleasant voice teases. It's Nate, on a walk past Jonas's house.

I blush. "Me. I'm talking to myself. Like a *grand-mère*, I am!"

"You don't look like a *grand-mère*," Nate teases and shakes his head.

I look desperately at him. How to answer what seems like a compliment? Shaking my head, "Not *grand-mère*, *oui!*" I stammer.

I want to say more, and ask about Jacques, but Nate calls back a goodbye and walks quickly to the front door of his workroom. So, I clutch a bowl of water and stagger towards Jonas's house. Abigail opens the door.

"Jonas is out," she says in French, nodding as if in encouragement. "He gets ready to go to the Northwest woods to cut wood." After Pegg makes us a hearty breakfast of eggs and sausage, Mistress seems stronger than she was last night.

At the end of the meal, Jonas rushes into the kitchen. He speaks quickly in English to Abigail. It's too fast. I don't understand.

Later, Abigail explains in French. "He wants me to go to Amagansett today to pick up old boards from the Fosters." She smiles at me, "Marie Josèphe lives with the Fosters, you know. So, I thought you'd like to drive the wagon."

"I'll be so happy if I see her! I'm glad to drive the wagon," I say.

Mistress Rose looks at Pegg, "Pegg, you will stay with the girls."

"Yes, Mistress," Pegg says.

Abigail nods, "that's good." Her voice is crisp, and she begins to direct Pegg and me to get ready. Abigail makes bread as I churn cream for butter. We will bring some gifts with us. The girls bring peas from the garden.

Pegg shells the peas, I suggest she boils them with mint, and add a big chunk of butter, for a light meal with fresh bread, instead of our usual dinner. We eat and are soon ready. It is about noon. Pegg has hitched up the wagon for us.

On the way, as the horse shuffles along the road, Abigail is quiet. The rough path runs along along beside the ocean past fields and marshes. Quacking ducks surge into the grey sky. Salty breezes brush my cheek, and my ears fill with the sound of waves crashing on the beach. It brings me back… I drift in memories of salt and sea in Acadia. Then I feel a hand on my arm. I turn, my eyes are cloudy with memories.

Abigail's soft green eyes look into mine. "Rose, if you had the freedom to come and go as you wish, what would you do?" she asks.

I am shaken and look away. "I do not know how far away Acadia is or where the other Acadians are," I say bitterly in French, "but I'd go back to Acadia, though I don't know what or who I would find there."

"That is so sad," she murmurs. Her face is quiet, almost like a mask. She gazes at the ocean waves. "Rose, I don't know if I can say this in French, but I will try. The waves roll endlessly," she says, "but I can never move." The tone of her voice is very sad.

"*Je ne comprends pas*," I say.

"You do understand, Rose. You know in your heart," she says.

Abigail rarely speaks like this. I turn and look at her. At Jonas's, I forget her feelings. She is just there: a woman soon to give birth, and I look at her only as that.

I hear her crying. Gently, I pull the horse to a stop and let her graze on the roadside, while turning to face Mistress.

Tears wet her cheek. She wipes them away. Leaning against the seatback, she turns away from me. Her dry sobs shake her body. I want to hold her, to comfort her, but I do not dare. Finally, she is quiet. When she turns back, her voice is a whisper.

"I will never sail off on those waves. My life will never leave these fields and this village. I have that feeling in my very bones, Rose. That I will never leave. Do you understand?"

"Mistress? You scare me," I mumble, secretly knowing what the Teacher told me, that Jonas had lost his affection for Abigail, that she came from off-island.

"You know what I mean, Rose. I know you know you do." Her voice softens. It is as if her voice is from another world, that she is a haunt and someone or thing speaks through her.

Nervously, I pick up the reins. The horse raises its head from the grass and looks back with a gentle, inquiring gaze. "Steady Star," I say gently. The horse drops its head to graze again. I drop the reins and clench my fingers in a ball so that I do not trouble the horse again and gather myself to listen well.

"Rose, my body is so heavy now. The birth could come any time. I fear for what happens then. I fear for myself and the little girls," Abigail says. "Like you, I am a stranger here. The women in town knew and liked Jonas's first wife. I do not feel bad about that. She was a good woman, I hear."

"But when I came, I was young and shy. I came from a big town, and I didn't know how to kill a chicken and do farm tasks like rendering fat from a pig carcass. I've tried to learn farm ways, but it's hard. And I'm so tired all the time that I don't visit much. The women may think that I don't want to be friends with them."

Why is she telling me all this? I cannot help her, but at least I can listen, which I know clears the spirit. Often, before, I shared my fears with Marie Josèphe and felt stronger later.

She looks out at the sea again then turns to me. "Do you think that you could stay on here, with Lydia and Phoebe, if anything happens to me?" Her green eyes look wise and infinitely sad. "Priscilla, just down the road, died in childbirth last summer. And Jonas can be... unfair. I know this may sound mad, but to whom can I go? And the little ones like you," she looks up and smiles crookedly.

"But I don't even think," I start to protest. Her eyes catch mine. I cannot escape the truth in them: this could happen to her. Pregnant women do die in childbirth. Herbs can help the pain. But if the baby's feet come first... or the bleeding is bad...

"Mistress," I start and then I cannot go on. I look at her and look out to the free sea, to the free waves that may have brushed the shores of Acadia.

I know, I want, to be on with my life. I want to leave here, with Pierre and Jacques and Marie Josèphe, to find my family, to make our own homes, in a new Acadia.

Abigail's eyes fix on me. As I hesitate, she says nothing. I still stay silent. I drop my eyes. And that is all that is said between us. But there is a deep bond here. I must be honest. I feel the pull of loyalty to her, not just as my mistress, but also as an older friend. But I cannot promise her to stay here.

We drive on down the rutted road. Abigail groans at the up and down bumps of the wagon... Then, finally, we are in Amagansett on the bluff road above the sea. Flocks of sheep pass us on the way back from pasture.

I gulp the clear, fresh air. Excitement about seeing Marie Josèphe makes my heartbeat faster. My heart sings. I am so happy, to be here, to be out of the house. And I will see my friend. What is new with her? Will we have time to find out? It is so hard not to see her.

Our horse ambles along. To the right, on the top of the dunes, beach plum and bayberry bushes grow beside the road. Pegg has told me their names. Far below the high dunes' path that we travel on, the ocean marches in soft waves to the beach. Small boats and fishnets lie on the sand.

To my left, small cottages sit, facing the ocean. "After two more houses, we are there," Abigail says.

I snatch another look at the ocean. A huge shape suddenly appears, beyond the white curly waves. Twin columns of water spout out of its body. Perhaps it is forty meters long. I know immediately that it's a whale. Whales and their calves swam into la Baie de Fundy off Acadia, and I saw them on the beach when they sometimes grounded.

As I watch, the whale rolls back and forth in the water; it looks like it might be sick. Perhaps, it is hurt.

"Look Mistress, a whale!" I say.

"A what?" Abigail says. "Oh," she says, her smile showing as she sees it too. She turns and says, "This is good. We're first. It's good. It's late in the season for whales now."

Her eyes are shining like I haven't seen them in weeks.

"Why is it good?" I ask.

"Since we're the first to see the whale, we'll get a reward! We get a half share in the proceeds, if it is caught," she says. "I must give the call "Whale Ho!" Abigail says. She grabs the reins from me, urges the old horse onto a fast trot, all the while yelling at the top of her voice, "WHALE HO!"

CHAPTER TWENTY-FIVE

WHALE HO!

In a minute, I see a woman on a small porch on the very top of her house yelling, "WHALE HO," and waving a piece of red cloth. Doors open, children run around screaming, "A whale! A whale!" The cries and noise all around me make me fear that our old horse will shy and run right over the bluff.

"Whale ho! Whale Ho!" Mistress keeps yelling. The horse goes faster. Men rush out of their little houses on the lane and race over the dune down to the ocean. Children scream and babies cry because of all the noise. Mistress still cries out "Whale ho!" but her voice grows weaker, and the horse slows to a jog-trot.

I don't know what I am supposed to do. The people seem to act on a plan that has been done before.

Our horse slows to a walk and a little crowd of women walks towards our wagon. "Mistress Abigail, you were the first!" A blond girl calls.

"Yes," she says and sits back down on the bench. "Rose," she whispers, "whatever I get for the whale bounty, I will give you half. Remember, Rose. It could help you." She reaches out to my hand and tugs on it.

"I will remember Mistress," I say. But in my heart, I wonder; will Jonas allow this?

We stop the wagon. Men rush by us carrying long oars, ropes and harpoons. Boys carry buoys to mark the whale if it dives. The men run down the bluffs to the beach, throw the buoys and oars into a whaleboat, pick the boat up and head for the ocean.

I steer the wagon to a clearing on the top of the bluff, between the wild roses. We can see the beach from here.

On the beach, six men jump into a boat. As they row, the boat slices sharply through the surf. A second whaleboat launches out from the beach, through the low breakers.

The whale, about twice the length of the boats, remains still. One boat is now twenty feet from the whale, a harpoon flies from the bowman's arm straight at the whale. It pierces its skin near its head. The rope between the boat and the whale snaps tight. It is strange as the whale does not run. It must be sick. The second whaleboat draws closer. A crewman stands erect, bends quickly stands and heaves; a lance that sticks into the whale's side.

Men scream as that boat flips, hit by the whale's tail. They stagger to shore as the whale runs for deep water, dragging the first whaleboat like a stick of wood.

If, as the whale gets farther offshore, the whale runs for deep water and dives below the the surface of the water, it will drag the whale boat behind. I have seen a whale do that in the Baie Fundaie. People die. I hold my breath. I cannot take my eyes off the struggle.

"WHALE HO!" Abigail stands up in the wagon and yells at the top of her voice. The horse moves out onto the road again. Why is she yelling now? I turn from the beach, confused. Abigail falls toward me. Her eyes are blank as if she has lost her senses. I struggle to hold the horse's reins. Her body sags into mine. It is heavy like a grain sack. I stagger, nearly falling out of the wagon. It is then that I notice drops of blood on the floor of the wagon.

"Are you all right?" I ask Abigail in a shaky voice.

Abigail mutters, "We must spread the news. We will get the re…ward." She is out of her mind.

I struggle to get the horse stopped. Little boys race up to see the horse. "Go! Go!" I scream. "Get Mistress Foster. Mistress Abigail is sick. "I pull off the road again, near bayberry bushes.

Around the corner of the second lane down from us, runs a Mistress, maybe Elizabeth Foster and Marie Josèphe. I try to hold the reins and wave. Star stands still now, her sides heaving.

Marie Josèphe runs up first. "Marie, she has gone faint," I gasp.

Abigail slumps on the seat. Marie Josèphe hops on the wagon and together, we hold Mistress in a sitting position. Mistress Foster helps. Marie Josèphe runs back to their cottage.

The men and boys still rush to the beach. They do not notice that Abigail has fainted. Shaken, I look at Abigail. Her eyes are open now. I read in them despair.

My heart breaks for her. I take her cold, limp hand. "I will take care of the girls, Mistress," I say. "Don't worry."

I hold her hand still, but my stomach sinks; I spoke too quickly.

Other women see us, come over and help. Mistress Foster holds Abigail's shoulders and Abigail's eyes flutter open. Her breath comes in short gasps. Her skin is pale and as I watch, she faints again.

I do not know if her peaceful rest is a good or bad sign.

"Make way!" Marie Josèphe screams as she races up to the wagon. When Abigail's eyes open again, Marie Josèphe holds a clay jug to her lips. Abigail takes a sip. Her eyes stay open. Mistress Foster speaks to Marie Josèphe. Marie Josèphe repeats her words to me in French, as Abigail slips in and out of awareness. "Abigail cannot go back. She must stay with Mistress Foster. Her house is just down the lane. Abigail may not now survive a cart ride to East Hampton."

I look at her wide-eyed as if I have never faced death before. Yet, I have sadly, many times on the ship. I try, then, to be calm. (I must be calm.)

Mistress Foster pats my hand as if she reads my thoughts. "You will be fine, Rose. I will send Marie Josèphe with you."

Mistress Foster calmly says, "We will take her to my house. Help us."

I squeeze her hand and look up. Abigail's eyes have closed. She is lifted onto a litter and carried down the road. Marie Josèphe goes with her, then returns to me.

I follow her to Mistress Foster's house. But as I settle our horse into their barn for a spell, I suddenly remember that I had finally promised Abigail that I would stay with her children if she died. Is my whole life to be spent in this English land? A deep pit opens in my spirit. Shivering with this thought, I go inside to help.

CHAPTER TWENTY-SIX

LOST FAMILY

After making Abigail comfortable at the Fosters, Marie Josèphe and I climb into Abigail's wagon and start back to East Hampton. Star ambles down to the end of the road on the bluff and I remember all that has just happened here. We stop and fill a gourd with water at the Indian Well. I steer Star to the rutted road to East Hampton.

The memory of Abigail, lying gasping on the ground, grey in the skin, haunts my thoughts. The old horse stumbles along. The shock of the day sits heavy on our shoulders.

"Oh my God, *c'est terrible*. Do you think she'll be all right? Lydia'll be so upset when Abigail doesn't come home."

My thoughts tumble out. I'm glad Marie Josèphe is here to share them. We're such good friends that we can be comfortable like this. Now so much has happened and still, we two are close in heart, I think.

"I long to hear your news, Marie Josèphe," I finally say. And trying to lift my spirits, I say, "It's good to speak in French."

"*Oui*," Marie Josèphe says. "Yes, I have much to tell. I found Pierre!"

"*Mon Dieu!*" My heart seems to spread joy from my head to my toes. "How?"

"He works for a fishing captain who lives in The Springs," she says. My Mistress ordered fish from the man, and Pierre brought it to Amagansett.

"How is he?" my heart beats pound in my chest.

"On the boat, they don't feed him much except fish, moldy potatoes and a rare carrot. He looks much older... But I can hug all around him now," Marie Josèphe chuckles softly.

"And, Rose, this is the other wonderful news. Pierre was delivering fish to a pier in Connecticut when he heard a man speak French like an Acadian. He too was taken to be a fisherman, and the man came from a place where Acadian have been settled in Connecticut. He says that there are people from Annapolis Royal there."

"Oh my God, Maman?"

"Pierre will try to find out more."

"I long to see him," I say. "*Mon Dieu*! What a day this has been; seeing the whale, seeing you for the first time in forever it seems, hearing that Pierre is close and now news that Maman and Madeleine may be alive!"

"We must pray now that Mistress Abigail's bleeding stops; God grant that she will live," Marie Josèphe says.

The shock of the day sits heavy on our shoulders, and we ponder our own thoughts on the way back to East Hampton. We are such good friends that we can be comfortable like this... It is so long since we two have been together. Now so much has happened and still we two are close in heart, I think.

"Rose, Pierre and I have talked," she quietly says.

I see a glow on her face, a warm look that tells me they are not just friends, but more than that. "I am glad," I say.

Marie Josèphe talks on, "Soon if we can do it, I want to try to escape with Pierre. We want to marry." She shakes her head. "How blessed we are that we found each other." Marie looks at me. "You know in a small village here, just as in Acadia, news travels quickly about a stranger in nearby villages."

Marie Josèphe's face glows, perhaps thinking of Pierre. She looks at me. "With all our fears, I'm treated well. So, I don't have to work too hard, and I think each day of when I might leave here. My family is kind but, this is not home."

"I'm so happy for you, Marie Josèphe," I say. "You know Maman always said that you two might marry."

"She did?" Marie Josèphe's face, broad forehead, and tanned cheeks touched with rose, light up with her smile. "Your Maman, my Maman, they knew most things, didn't they, Rose?"

"They did, they did. We just didn't listen to them enough," I say with a quiet laugh.

"And do you think of your fine André?" she asks gently.

"I do more these days. But where can he be and is he still alive? Could it be that he is in Connecticut?"

"We must have faith, Rose, you know that" she says.

"I know, I know. Still, a young man in town, tries to speak to me. He is a new friend."

"Perhaps more than a friend, eh?" she asks.

"I do not know."

But now Marie Josèphe is in love, and she knows Pierre loves her. And my André is lost to me so I'm not sure how I feel.

We sit quietly. The sun lights the leaves on the trees. Star plods along, her head sunk. A few sheep in the meadow baa hopefully for food as they hear our wagon creak by.

"Marie Josèphe, I fear for Abigail," I say. "I truly feel in my heart that she and the children may suffer if I leave now. Before I came here, I did not think that I could care about anyone English."

"I cannot see things the way you do, but we'll work together, my friend, like the old times? Yes?" She laughs heartily and repeats, "We work together we two, yes?"

"*Oui*," I say, "we work together."

She lays a hand on my knee. "Now," she says briskly, "we must help out with Abigail's family as much as we can."

"Yes, Lydia and Phoebe will be sad that their Maman has not returned."

"You want to help everyone, Rose, except yourself!" Marie Josèphe shakes her head.

Hoof beats sound ahead… Star perks up her ears and Jonas appears on the road ahead.

When he gets near us, he waves to us to stop. "What has happened? Why isn't Abigail with you?" he demands.

I tell him what happened. He doesn't understand. "Rose, you must go back and get Mistress Abigail. Abigail must come home."

"Mistress Abigail is weak, Master," I say. "She cannot be moved. She may die."

Jonas's face turns white. "Where is she?" he demands.

Marie Josèphe speaks up, "She is with Mistress Foster."

Jonas drops his head and mumbles, "Go on to East Hampton. I will come when I can." He jerks on his horse's reins, hits him with a stick and gallops off towards the Foster's.

Just then, the sharp cries of boys playing a game, distract me. They toss a ball in a small field. Marie Josèphe pokes me, "That looks like Jacques there," she says.

The boy has black hair, and he is light on his feet. He runs and stops and throws the ball with a snap to his arm. Yes!

"Jacques!" We both call.

He turns and runs towards us. We see his rosy cheeks, his mop of wild black hair escaping from under his cap. He runs effortlessly beside our slow wagon.

"Jacques! *Ça va?*"

"I am well," says Jacques. The other boys run up to me. "This is my sister," he says to them in English.

"Mistress Rose is your sister?" A slim boy with spectacles calls. "Your sister is a servant!" He starts a sing song. The other boys join in, "Your sister is a ser-vant. Your sister is a servant!"

Jacques's fist hits the boy's face so hard that his glasses fly off and his nose bleeds.

"Oh, Jacques." I stop the wagon.

"?... *C'est stupide*," Jacques yells.

Screams split the air. The other boys pile on top of Jacques but he scrambles around and punches them. Marie Josèphe and I don't know what to do.

"Stop this fighting!" a deep voice calls.

Nate saunters down the rise from the cemetery. He pulls the boys off Jacques as if he is lifting branches.

"Mistress Rose," he says, looking at me and holding Jacques, "This is a friend of yours. Yes?"

"Yes, Nate, my brother."

"Boys!" He smiles and shrugs his big shoulders.

I smile back at him. "Thank you for helping him."

Nate puts Jacques down. He walks over to our wagon and leans against it. Star feels the weight and shifts her feet, bobbing her head. Nate looks up at me. His voice is quiet so that the little boys will not hear.

"How are things with you, Rose?" he asks. I do understand. But my English is not good enough to answer. So, I shrug my shoulders.

Jacques quickly cries out, "Rose."

"No," Nate says firmly.

"Someday, Jacques, we will go," Marie Josèphe says firmly to Jacques. "We will go away." Marie Josèphe adds, "Go, child, with your Master, now."

Nate stares at her but says nothing. "Mistress Rose," he says. "I hope to talk to you again soon." He looks at me anxiously, "Do you understand, Rose?"

My eyes flicker cautiously to Nate's. I see his steady open gaze. "Yes, Nate." In the falling darkness, it is impossible to know exactly what he means, but I nod my head...

He stops walking beside the wagon drops back and waves goodbye.

Marie Josèphe whispers in French, "You do like him, Rose?"

"I don't know him really well," I throw my hands in the air and let the reins flop.

"There's Pegg!"

"Welcome home, Mistress Rose," Pegg calls in her lilting voice. The words touch my heart.

CHAPTER TWENTY-SEVEN

PROMISE TO MARIE JOSÈPHE

Lydia flies out the door. "Rose, what has happened? Where are Mama and Papa? Why are you here without Mama? Who is that with you?" Her voice shakes and I know from her quick words how worried she is. As I step down from the wagon, Lydia throws herself at me, grabbing me around my skirt. I can feel the desperately tight grip of her arms. I try to hug her and turn her face up to mine. I smooth her hair, "Lydia, Lydia, I am here. I'll be with you," I murmur.

She stands back from me. "I don't want you here," she wails. "I want my Mama. Why didn't you bring her with you? Where is Papa?"

Light falls on her face and I see suspicion in her eyes. "Come, Lydia." I try to take her hand. She pulls away. I don't know what to say.

Phoebe stands beside the house door. She won't come out of the house. I walk up to the door. I look down at her and her eyes are red from crying and she has a large dirt smudge on her cheek.

"Lydia is mean to me, Rose. And she's not nice to Pegg, and," Phoebe cries, "I want my Mama. Why did you take her away?"

I don't know what to do or say. The girls desperately want their mother. And I worry so much about Abigail. I cannot show that to them. I do not want to scare them. And I don't know what Jonas has told them.

I try to pull the girls to sit down with me on a bench. They do not want to be near me.

Marie Josèphe comes in from putting Star in the barn. Pegg whispers to me, "Mistress, have baby?" I put a finger to my mouth.

"Not yet, Pegg. She fell down... and is very weak."

Pegg nods. "When she comes, I take good care of baby, Mistress Rose," she says with a smile. And I know she will. Pegg has a gentle way. Quietly, Pegg puts bread and butter on the table.

I sink down on a bench near the table and slather butter on hunks of bread to give to the children. Lydia stands at the end of the table and glares at me. "Papa said that you did not take care of Mama. He says that maybe she fell out of the wagon and hit her head because you were driving too fast," Lydia says.

I try to answer her gently. It is so like Jonas to think the worst of me. "No, Lydia," I say. "Listen to me. This is what happened," I say. I tell the girls the story of the discovery of the whale in the water off Amagansett Beach. "Mama was so brave, calling out, 'Whale Ho.'" The two small faces look at me.

Lydia repeats, "My Mama is brave. She told me to be brave too. I remember that now," her lilac-blue eyes drift as she remembers.

"After Mama saw the whale, she must have felt sick, so she fainted," I finish.

"You mean that her eyes closed?" Phoebe asks.

"Yes, it was like that. She felt sick and dizzy in her head." I think it best not to tell them about her blood on the quilt.

"So Mistress Foster took Mama home and she will take good care of her for a day or so, until she can come home," I say.

The girls relax a little and nibble at bread and butter and when they finish, I ask, "Are you ready to go to bed, now?"

"After a story, and if you come with us and hear our prayers," Lydia says. Pegg lights a whale oil lamp to shed more light and Marie Josèphe tells the girls a funny

Acadian story which she can translate into English. It is about a crow that outwits a wolf. The girls giggle and laugh. Then, I go with the girls to their beds and listen to their prayers.

We pray for Mama and the new baby she will deliver soon, and we pray that Papa will come home safe. Even with my bad feelings towards Master Jonas, I am able to pray for him with the girls. This is a family, I see, and love is here in the little girls' hearts. Finally, the girls drop off to sleep in the little room off the kitchen.

I walk out to the kitchen and Pegg hands me a cup of clam soup. The warm rich creamy soup, filled with clam bits and potatoes and carrots and onions fills my stomach and warms my spirit.

The fire is banked for the night but glows warm and hot and Marie Josèphe sits in the corner at Abigail's wheel. She spins wool from the fleece in the basket at her feet.

Pegg stands for a moment at the bottom of the ladder to the sleeping loft. Her small face is almost hidden in the dark. But I see her dark eyes fixed on me. In her soft voice, she says, "When Mistress Abigail comes home, I brew my ginger tea, make her strong."

"That's good, Pegg. She will need that," I agree.

"Good night, Mistress Rose," she says.

"Good rest, Pegg," I wish her.

Pegg climbs upward. I hear her moving about on the attic floor and then silence.

Marie Josèphe carefully removes the spindle of wool thread that she has woven on the large spinning wheel. She looks expectantly at me.

"I wonder how Abigail is now. God grant that she recovers from this weakness," I say. We both sit quietly. A log crumbles with a hiss and a soft thud. "I pray she lives... she just cannot die," I say. I look over at Marie Josèphe. Our eyes meet.

"Yes, she could die. You know that and I do, too," Marie Josèphe says.

"We must think of ourselves, Rose," she says firmly. "We must make plans."

"I know. I know," I say. "Are you sure that André is across the bay?" I ask and through my mind race images of our last night together, the night he asked me to leave Acadia with him and his Acadian mother. Those days are hazier, less heart moving now, but there they are.

"Mama!" I hear Phoebe call out in her sleep and put a finger to my lips as I look at Marie Josèphe.

Her dark eyes hold mine. We look at each other and sit in silence. There is another moan as one of the girls dreams. Then, silence.

Marie Josèphe speaks quietly and urgently in French. She says, "Listen to me Rose! Now that Pierre knows that Acadians are in Connecticut, he works on a plan to get us there. He is sure that Acadians from Annapolis Royal were unloaded at New London. There is more than one family in a village called Guilford and there might be members of your own family. The Acadians are not free to leave Guilford. But they can work as they need and are not mistreated. And a group of them have their own house to live in. If we had others to help plan, maybe we all could get back to Acadia, Rose. Pierre wants you to come with us and help you escape."

"Is Pierre sure those Acadians came from Annapolis-Royal villages?" I ask.

"They probably are but even if they are not, they are Acadians, he does not know much yet," Marie Josèphe admits. "He is trying to learn more. But he says that even now it is getting colder, and Bay waters can toss a fishing boat like a leaf. If we want to cross the Bay in a boat to reach Guilford, we do not have much time." Marie Josèphe's voice is deep and full. "Travel in a small boat can be treacherous and that's probably the way we'll have to travel. If we can get a local man to take us." She takes my twisting hands between her warm ones, looks me in the face and asks, "You will come, Rose?"

"How can we get a boat to take us and how can we get to it, without someone seeing us?" I ask loud and bold, knowing this is a time to use a loud voice.

Marie Josèphe's voice drops. "I don't know. But Pierre has talked to the schoolteacher, Sarah's father. You know him. He lives near Accabonac Harbor, and he might get a boatman to get us across the Sound. It is not a long voyage, but the wind can make it a treacherous trip to Conn-nect-ti-cut."

She laughs, "Ah, these words are hard to say." She is quiet. Then looking at a small silver bowl on a shelf, says, "You could take that bowl to pay a boatman."

I shake my head. "I cannot steal that bowl. It is Abigail's. Her mother brought it with her from England to Connecticut and she brought it here when she married Jonas. I cannot steal her most precious possession."

"Yes," Marie Josèphe says, "You can do that! You are kept here against your will. You have the right to be free."

Marie Josèphe's voice is low, but it burns into my heart.

I have the right to be free, Yes! But stealing Abigail's bowl…

"After a night's sail, we will be again with our Acadians. Can you see this, feel what that will be like?"

"Yes, yes! I remember… We can all chat away in our own language. We can call out to the little one's as they play around us and speak with love to the elders as they sit knitting away at the table. We can EAT!" I stop, then say, thinking of fricot, "clam fricot, chicken fricot, trout fricot…"

Marie Josèphe butts in laughing, "even weasel fricot!" And I have to laugh, too, about the fricot made just with potatoes, 'because the weasel ran away.'

Marie Josèphe says, "You will be ready, then, when I get word to you, to escape?"

"Yes, of course. But," I shake my head and then drop it into my hands, "I never believed that I could worry about Abigail. But I do. She is very weak. Even if the English betrayed us, I need to care for her. In Acadia, we do not leave people in trouble."

"Rose, come to your senses! Even if you don't steal the bowl, Pierre and I leave. Then, you are alone here in this village. You may never in your life see me again, see Pierre again. We will try to take Jacques with us. You will be alone here. Where is your loyalty, your heart? Is trying to find your own mother not more important than a sick English woman? What if your mother is across the water? And you do not see her?"

"Stop, stop! I know, I know and, what if André is there? Is he still the man that I see in my dreams? Or was I just a young girl then, who wanted to marry because my blanket was near done. I don't know any of these things." I drop my head into my hands and try to hold back tears.

"But you would be free, Rose. Free!"

"No, not as you say it. We would all still be prisoners."

"We Acadians would be together in Connecticut. Not torn apart as we are in New York." Marie Josèphe's voice trembles and drops so that I can hardly hear the French words she speaks. We sit and watch the fire sink into embers.

It is night, the wind blows outside. I think of Abigail, when will the baby be born, will it be alive…

"I need time," I say. "If Abigail gets back here alive, if she recovers strength, I will do it. Abigail told me that she would try to give me one-half of her whale money. That could pay the boatman."

Marie Josèphe looks at me. A long look: she seems to see into my head. She nods her head, slowly. "I believe you," she says. "And I pray for her speedy recovery."

CHAPTER TWENTY-EIGHT

THE ROCKING CHAIR

Marie Josèphe wakes next to me in the attic. It is good to have her here, especially since Jonas is gone and we can speak French.

"I dreamt of Pierre. He is out on the sea on a fishing boat now. I never stop worrying... you know what can happen," she says.

"I do." I do not want to say more.

Both of us know men who have been swept off in fishing boats, fishing boats that have foundered in heavy seas. It happened in Acadie. Since I have been here, I heard about a boat that went down in a ferocious storm in the ocean off Montauk.

At breakfast, when she hears Marie Josèphe and me speaking French, Lydia doesn't like it, "Rose, what are you two talking about?" she pouts.

"You know how you talk with your best friend… that's what we do," I say. "Marie Josèphe is my friend since we were little girls like you and lived in a village in Acadie."

"Rose! How did you get here? Where is Acadie?" Lydia asks. "I remember once you were in the village square here and everyone was staring at you." Her voice is puzzled. "I felt bad for you… then. And then, Maman did not tell us anything about you. She just said that you were here to help."

Marie Josèphe tries to explain, "Lydia, your Rose once lived in a village like you. But then she was put on a ship and sailed across the ocean till she came here."

"But why is she here? Why did she leave her Mama and village and end up in our village? Why is she here and Mama isn't?" Lydia's face twists up and she sobs.

I reach my arms to her and she lets me hold her. "Lydia, Lydia, someday I will explain to you," I say.

"Don't!" Lydia pulls away from me.

"Where is Mama?" Phoebe bursts out. "She has been away so long."

"She has not, goose. She just left yesterday," Lydia tries to comfort her sister but her voice shakes. She turns to me, "Rose, why hasn't she come back?"

"Remember that your Mama and I went to Amagansett? Mama got sick there. She had to stay with Mistress Foster. …She may even have had her new baby by now."

"Baby!" Phoebe shrieks. "Will she have the new baby when she comes home?"

Just then, we hear a scrabbling scratch on the door, and it bursts open and a little boy races in from the yard. "Your Papa and Mama are coming!" he calls.

"Come on!" Phoebe pulls my hand. Lydia races ahead of us. We rush into the yard, and I stumble over wagon wheel ruts and feel a jabbing pain in my ankle.

Star trots slowly up to the gate. Jonas holds the reins tightly to stop the horse from rushing to the stable. A hooded figure leans against Jonas. It must be Abigail.

Lydia opens the gate latch and struggles to push the gate open. I hobble over to help her. Jonas climbs down. He walks up beside Star and pulls back on the mare's head to bring her to a gentle stop.

"Can you walk, Abigail?" he calls.

A muffled voice answers, "Can you take the baby?"

Jonas takes a tiny bundle from Abigail. Then he helps her down. She moves as if she does not want to hurt herself.

Jonas puts one arm around Abigail's shoulders, and with the other arm, holds the baby in the crook of his arm. Abigail can hardly put one foot in from of the other. But Jonas holds her firmly.

I have not seen Jonas take care of Abigail before. I wonder if this new birth has touched his heart?

Lydia jumps up to hug Abigail and Abigail lurches against Jonas. He calls out sharply, "Girls! Mama is not well, yet. Let me help her into the house."

Marie Josèphe has followed us out of the house. She and I exchange glances: Abigail's skin color is yellow, and she doesn't seem to be able to stand up straight.

Inside the house, Abigail sinks onto a bench. She holds the baby up so we can see it. Phoebe picks up a corner of the swaddling blanket and wraps it around the tiny dangling legs that have escaped from the fold. The baby is like a little doll," she whispers to me, "so small." I try to rub her back gently. "Yes," I say.

"What is wrong with Mama?" Lydia asks.

Jonas sits down on the bench by the fire. He glances at Abigail huddled beside him and puts an arm around her shoulder. "I will speak simply to them, wife," he says.

Abigail's voice sounds like a croak when she nods up and down and says, "Yes, Jonas."

Jonas clears his throat. His eyelids droop with fatigue. "I hope that Mama will be well, soon," he says, "But she had a hard time having the baby. She nearly died. She must rest now or she and the baby might get very sick."

Jonas puts one hand on each side of Lydia's face and looks into her eyes, "I hope Mama soon will be fine, child," he says.

Abigail barely moves her head in agreement. Jonas's honesty and the raw news that Abigail nearly died, shocks me and a shiver runs through my body. Might she have died? This is too much for me to take in. I fear for her more, now. How could I possibly leave her? I drop my eyes.

Phoebe sobs quietly. "Mama cannot die!" she says.

Lydia soberly wraps her arms around her and murmurs, "Phoebe, Phoebe, we will take care of Mama."

Jonas is silent for a moment... and I see glimpses of pain and resolve cross his face... "We must ask the Lord for His blessing," he says and drops his head. He grabs one hand of each girl and when he raises his head, he smiles at Abigail. They pray together.

"I do not feel strong enough to go upstairs," Abigail says. "Phoebe and Lydia, do not worry, soon I will feel better." I hear her voice fading from fatigue and hope she will be better…

"It is so good to be home," she says. "Help me to the bed off the kitchen, Rose. I will nurse the baby there and sleep."

I feel her body shaking and she leans so heavily against me that I can hardly hold her up. I help her lie down on the feather mattress and hand her the baby. She puts him to her breast and in a moment both of them are fast asleep.

Jonas sinks on a bench near the table and drops his head in his hands. He takes a deep breath and looks up. "Let's make a little game," Jonas says. "If one of you guesses the baby's name, she'll get an extra piece of Pegg's apple pie. Fair?"

"Fair," Lydia says with bright eyes.

Lydia and Phoebe try a few different names; Robert and Israel and Jethro and then Lydia calls out, "Caleb."

"Well, you both can ask Pegg for an extra piece," Jonas smiles. "His name is Caleb, and he is a little boy, even for a baby... You see that he has red hair like Maman," Jonas says softly. "Later, you can see him again and maybe hold him."

Pegg quietly puts slabs of apple pie on the table, with beer for Jonas and cider for the girls and me. After a few minutes, Jonas says, "Rose, I bring word from Mistress Foster that Marie Josèphe must go back to Amagansett."

"Yes, Master. She is feeding the animals. I will go out to the barn and tell her."

As I walk across the ground, I feel that the air is getting colder. The winds blow fierce out of the northeast today. Pierre will want to get away soon, I think. I want to hear more of Pierre's plans from Marie Josèphe. But now she must leave. I meet her on the path.

"Sarah and her father are trying to get a boat to take you across the Bay to New London," she says. 'That's the best place to land, for fisherman often go there to sell fish."

"Keep your ears open, Rose," she adds. "And remember that Abigail's silver bowl could pay our passage across the water to Connecticut."

"No," I murmur.

"You must!" Marie Josèphe urges, and then we are at the house.

Marie Josèphe opens the kitchen door and asks, "You sent for me, Master?"

"Yes!" Jonas says and turns towards her. "Mistress Bellows has asked for you to return to her in Amagansett. If you leave now and walk quickly, you should reach there by nightfall."

"Yes, Master," Marie Josèphe says.

She walks to the attic stairs. I go beside her and she pulls me close. She whispers, "I will try to get news to you. Your friend Nate also knows that Pierre hopes to escape. If you see Sarah or Nate on the green, try to talk to them." She goes up the stairs, comes down with a satchel and leaves without looking back.

I hardly know where to look, what to do, what to think. Without Marie Josèphe here my Acadian world vanishes. And Abigail's weakness scares me.

How could I ever have guessed that this family, this place, would steal its way into my heart. I do care for them, and yet, my heart longs even more to be with my own Acadians. I stand still, alone, groggy with care.

"Rose, Rose, look what Pegg made… see!" Phoebe holds a tiny woven sheet and a blue knitted blanket.

"It is beautiful," I say softly.

Pegg lifts a big black pot from the hearth. She smiles at me. Few nice words come to her ears; I know.

"Go out and get a log, Phoebe," she says, "to keep the fire strong."

.

CHAPTER TWENTY-NINE

THE ROCKING CHAIR

Phoebe dashes back into the house... "Papa! Nate is coming to see you! He carries a big chair. He says it is for Mama. Is it? Is it? Is it for her and the baby?"

"Yes, It is for Mama and the baby," Jonas says.

Pegg looks up from the stove and our eyes meet. We are both surprised. This is a kind gift, not something that Jonas might usually do. But in his words as well, he seems happy about his new child.

I open the door for Nate. "Where shall I put it?" he asks.

From the fireside, Jonas beckons to Nate. "Nate, put the chair down so I can look at it," he says softly so as not to wake Abigail who is sleeping in the little room. Jonas runs his hand over the smooth wood, looks carefully at the joints and pushes, to set the chair rocking.

"It is good work, Nate, well worth what I paid you," he says.

Nate shifts from one foot to another. "Thank you, Master."

"Take it upstairs," Master says. "When Abigail feels better, she will use it, I know... Now, I have much work to do."

"I will show you where to put the chair," I tell Nate.

Nate follows me up the narrow stairs, carrying the chair. He stumbles, dropping it.

I turn around.

"Worse than a balky calf," he grunts.

"Can I help?"

He shakes his head, picks up the chair and staggers into the bedroom.

We both pause and look around: Nate is short of breath. I am surprised. The few times that I had been in this room before were at night. I could only see Abigail's face in the bed... I did not realize then what a pleasant room it is.

A fire burns low on the grate. Pegg must have set it early, a large bed, covered with stuffed coverlets has two large pillows on top, covered in snowy linen. A colorful rag rug and neat spinning wheel fill the room. The two gable windows on the east side let in soft light.

"Put the chair here by the east gable windows," I say. "The baby can watch the flickering light through the tree branches when he is burped."

"Burped?" Nate smiles at the word. "Mistress Rose, you know about babies?"

I half-smile, thinking of my Acadian life, "Oh Yes, Nate."

Nate's blue eyes are warm. I feel his closeness, smell his sweat. When I look at him, I feel shaky although I don't know why.

Nate's broad shoulders and his height seem even bigger in this bedroom with a low ceiling.

Nate has never looked at me like he is now. My cheeks feel warm. Even though he seems close, I do not step back. Nate puts out his hand and grasps one of mine. I feel the rough strength of it. My hands tremble.

"Mistress Rose, I have to speak fast. I hope you understand me," he says in a solemn voice.

I lift my eyes. "What is it Nate? I think I will understand you," I say glancing nervously at the door, "my English lessons with Sarah go well."

"You know that Pierre and Marie Josèphe will try soon to get to New London?"

"I have heard that just today, Nate," I say.

"But what about you, Rose? Are you going as well?" Nate's eyes, calm, and kind, fix upon mine.

"Mistress knows nothing of the plan. But earlier she asked me to stay. And I fear for her life. She is very weak... I don't know Nate." I stumble with my words.

"Will you think to stay here, for a time, so that we can know each other?" Nate's deep voice is clear.

"Nate, I..."

Nate suddenly smiles, "Rose?"

"I know this is sudden, Rose. But I have to speak now."

The sun slides in the dormer windows. And then I feel my wits return. I struggle to get the right English words. "Nate, I cannot... say for sure. We have so few minutes here."

"Rose. Time is short. Pierre may leave soon," Nate says. He speaks as if he struggles to control himself. "But, I will wait," he finally says.

"Rose!" Jonas's heavy voice blasts up the stairs. "Hurry down here!"

"Yes, Master," I step away from Nate. Shocked speechless, I follow him downstairs.

Nate turns, "I must go," he says

Suddenly I am aware of the chill in the room. The fire has burned down to embers.

Nate's feet tramp across the kitchen. He turns, our eyes meet, and he leaves.

CHAPTER THIRTY

THE FIRE KINDLES

This morning, I try to start the fire. Pegg's outside gathering wood when I hear a soft knock. I'm on my knees on the stone hearth, reaching back into the fireplace. Fire glimmers in the rosy ash, at the back of the hearth. I hear a soft knock. I cannot get up or look back. I am trying to get the fire to burn.

"Good morning," I hear Nate say from the doorway. I cannot scramble out to meet him. The fire is too important.

"Morning, Nate," I mumble.

I hear him dragging a bench to sit down. "Can I help?" he asks.

"No!" I say more positively than I mean. I am so desperate about the fire going out, that I cup one hand near the glowing embers. I drop dry seaweed onto the embers. The tiny branches catch. "Well, Yes!" I say, "There is more dry seaweed in the tinder box."

A second or so later, I feel his hand bump against mine in the ashes. He opens his palm and tendrils of dry seaweed fall out.

"More!" I beg. Again, I feel him push his arm down alongside my body, to reach the tiny flames. The feeling of his arm on my body is good.

More tiny flames light. Nate pushes more small twigs from the kindling box, past my body. The fire grows. I must get out, or I will get burned.

Cramped and dusty, I painfully pull my knees up off the stone hearth and stand up. Since I am a few inches shorter than he, Nate looks down at me. I can see his smile, but I can also see that he tries not to laugh at me. Perhaps I have soot on my nose?

"Stay here and keep it going," I mumble and escape to the attic where I have a clean apron and I can wipe off my face. Then I come down the stairs.

Nate is still sitting patiently by the hearth, feeding the fire with seaweed and branches. He has smudges of soot on his face and in his hair.

"It is lit," he says. "The big log flames." He stands and leans against the wall by the hearth.

"Rose?" he asks with a smile. "Your English is good now, isn't it? I need you to know everything I say, now."

"Not good, not bad," I say, returning the smile. "Sit with me for a minute."

I plop down on the fireside bench beside him. "Nate, I am still thinking about what you asked me," I say. "But Nate, I, today, don't know what to answer," I stammer.

"That is all right, Rose," He looks into the fire seeing the flames leap up blue at the base and yellow and red. He looks at me. "Rose, I just want you to see that in this village, we are much like the people from your old village. We farm. We fish. We go to church. We love our families. Even though there is a struggle going on between the French and the English, you could live happily with me."

I sigh. "Yes, but my life before… it seems years and years ago... Then we were the same. But we Acadians have lost everything except each other. We have lost our freedom and our home. It's different when you are like me, stuck in a place and life not by my own choice, without anyone of my own here. It is hard to decide anything when one has lost the power to choose: whether to go out to the beach or stay in the yard to pound samp. It changes you. It changes me. I don't know how to say, really. But it changes your insides like you are standing in water and feel like flowing sand, washed back and forth by the water, not steady on your own legs."

"I know it is hard for you, Rose. But it is hard for me, too. Can you think about staying here with me?

The way his blue eyes settle on mine, the way he speaks, the kind way he treats Jacques, I see that, and it catches my heart. "Nate, you are a good man," I stammer.

"Rose, I have never spoken for another, ever," he says. His cheeks redden. "But when I heard of Pierre and Marie Josèphe's plan to escape, I guessed you might leave with them. I know we know little of each other. I cannot hold you, can hardly talk to you, but there is something about you, a spirit away, that wins my heart. There was no other time, but now, to ask. My father may not be pleased about my asking you. We might have to leave this town." His voice drops to a husky murmur. "But I hope you will stay with me."

"Nate, my heart is close to yours. In this short, strange time, this has happened, and Oh god, I do not know what to do!"

Nate stands closer to me. Our eyes meet.

"I have good skills. I can support us with my carpentry, watchmaking, and farming," he says. "And my uncle lives near the Hudson River and has extra land. We could move there if you were not comfortable here."

I had had some thought that Nate liked me. I am fifteen now and certainly like being liked. But truly I didn't know the depth of his feelings. What can I say, do, that won't hurt this man I have come to treasure.

He holds out his arms and I fall into them as a port in the storm of my feelings. Then kissing him on the cheek, I back away and stand silent.

Finally, my feelings brim over into tears and yet I know I have to speak.

"Nate, in Acadie a young man asked me to leave Acadie with him before we were all put on the ships. It was when we learned we must all leave Acadie. I thought I was in love with him, but I said that I was young and… and not… that I wasn't sure enough about us to leave my family and go with him. That my family needed me."

I stand up and look away from Nate, remembering. "Life was so different there, so simple, we all knew pretty much what we were going to do, that we would marry one of our own Acadians and live there forever. Now, my life is…."

"After that terrible day when you were thrown on the ships and sailed away from Acadia, nothing is the same," Nate finishes my sentence.

"It is true, nothing is the same. I have no roots here. And I like having roots and sinking into a life where I know people and I am one of them. Now there is a chance that Acadian people from our town, perhaps he and my Maman are in Connecticut. I want to find out."

Nate shakes his head. "There is no way you can find out quickly… If Pierre can get a boat, he will try to leave very soon. He will want you to come with him. He wants to take Jacques as well. Probably a day or so is all the time that we have."

My hand reaches out… He covers it with his.

"I am sorry to be slow in my answer, Nate. I care for you," I say and my voice trembles.

"Jacques is like my own little brother. He could stay with us," he says.

"Nate, Jacques may wish to go with Pierre," I say, "and I," I turn away for a moment to gather myself, "I need to know about my Acadians. I cannot decide if I do not know."

"I pray that you will stay. But I will wait for your decision. Now, I must talk to Master Jonas. I have important news for his ears. Jonas's son was found alive near Albany. He may be free soon to come home to East Hampton."

Caleb's cry breaks into the moment.

"Nate," I half-turn around to go upstairs and get the baby from Abigail.

"I must leave now," Nate says. He walks to the door and closes it quietly.

CHAPTER THIRTY-ONE

THE LADIES GOSSIP

That day, I fry buckwheat crepes and we add maple syrup for a light supper. As we eat, I feel a cold chill of wind rush in alongside one of the windows. The seaweed stuffing falls to the floor. Wind moans and surges against the house with sheets of rain. Even here in the North Village, I hear the ocean surf crashing on the beach. The waves must be huge, cresting far out, pounding on the beach and destroying the dunes. And in Peconic Bay, the waters may be very rough.

Loving Nate, talking with Nate, the thought of being with him makes me happy. I don't know what to do. I also want to leave with Pierre and Marie Josèphe and Jacques if Abigail recovers. And we may find that Maman, Madeleine and André are alive in Guilford, or we may not.

Master Jonas rushes in from the yard. Nate has told him about his son, Ephraim. An important matter has come up about the boy, he says, he must go to New York

City as soon as he can find a boat to sail him there. He goes upstairs to speak to Abigail and leaves.

Abigail comes down with the baby and nibbles at a crêpe. "Did you hear the news about Ephraim?" she asks me.

"Yes," I say quietly. A log snaps in a shower of sparks, and I come back to this moment. After the meal, I see a pile of raw wool in the lean-to and go to the spinning wheel and spin.

Pegg leaves to feed and milk the cow. She comes in with a bucket full of milk and a message for Abigail. "Some village women are at the gate. They ask if they can come to see you and the baby."

Abigail nods yes. Quickly, she takes her cap off to primp her limp hair and puts it back on. Four ladies open the door, stamp their feet outside and come into the kitchen. A blast of cold air chills the room and Abigail covers the baby's face.

"Oh, may we see him?" a chubby woman asks. "Why he is a tiny one," she says, holding the baby's fingers in hers.

"He is," Abigail says, "But he sucks well. He cries loud." She smiles, "my sleep is little these days."

Two women settle themselves on a bench in front of the sitting-room fire. Pegg and I bring the other two women a bench to sit on. The women loosen their shawls, one has a baby and she puts it to her breast to nurse. I bring in a chair for Abigail. She sits and looks at her friends.

"It's so good to see you. So much has happened so fast," she says. She cuddles Caleb to her chest, and he falls asleep. "Talk, please talk, while he sleeps," she chuckles.

Temperance, the chubby young wife of Joshua, a ship owner starts, "I borrowed the latest newspaper that Joshua has from New York City. Abigail. Could you read us some of it?"

"I will," Abigail says with the first bright smile I have seen in weeks. She glances over the pages then reads a bit aloud. While she reads different bits of news, one woman takes out a quilt square and sews. Another knits a sweater.

"Our wood is near gone, again," one says.

Then Abigail folds the journal broadsheet. "Our army has pulled back from northern New York to Fort Edward near Albany, for the winter," she reads.

I am glad now that Sarah has taught me quite well. I understand quite a few English words now.

"I wish this war had never started," the old widow from down the street says. "Since all our beef is sent to the troops, I have to eat corn samp and fish, day after day."

The ladies agree and talk more. They seem good friends and I remember Maman's friends visiting like this to catch up on the news. Then, they lower their voices. "That girl is French, isn't she. Abigail? The French have killed boys from Southampton, even this year."

I look up just in time to overhear another woman say, "I don't see how you can trust her in the house and with the children."

Temperance, the chubby one, glances at me. Her face is like a china dollface I saw once: blue eyes peer out from blond curls. But her voice is firm. "Be fair to her, ladies. Rose is not French. She is an Acadian who speaks French. English soldiers took her from her home in Acadia and brought her here."

"I've heard tell that the French want to make us all papists," the miller's wife says.

"But she is not one of the French, "Abigail protests.

My hands tremble on the spinning wheel. I get up and stir and knead bread to hide my distress.

Although I have moved out of their sight, I hear Temperance speak up. "Listen to me, ladies, Rose, and her brothers got caught up in the middle of the war between England and France."

"I feel weak now, ladies, maybe you should go," Mistress Abigail says.

With clucks to little Caleb and goodbyes to Abigail, the women prepare to leave. Temperance moves close and speaks slowly in English to me, "It is true that some of us think like that woman, but most do not!" she says

I bob my head towards her, "*merci*, my friend." My heart is pounding.

After the last woman leaves, Abigail turns to me. "Oh Rose, I feel warm and sick to my stomach. Maybe I did too much." She slumps in her chair and closes her eyes.

"I feel like I am on fire," she whispers through parched lips. She points to her throat. "I cannot swallow. It hurts."

I see tears in Abigail's eyes. "I'm scared," she says. "Jonas is not here, and I feel very sick. My bones ache, my teeth ache. There is a throat sickness about that killed two women already."

I try to stay calm but am terrified myself. "Should I get one of the women?" I ask. "I do not know much about sickness."

"Let us get through the day," she says, "and see how I am."

"Yes, Mistress."

I help her upstairs to her bedroom and settle her into bed. And as I step back from the bed, I live again that moment when Nate and I placed the chair in this room, and he asked me to stay here in East Hampton.

I must decide. It is not fair to him... Tonight, I am no closer to an answer.

CHAPTER THIRTY-TWO

ROSE ALONE

"Something to drink! Make chamomile tea and give it to me. I must drink," Abigail cries.

"Yes, *oui*, it takes time to make it, Abigail." I am very nervous and unsure and as I rush to get the fire stirred up and hot water boiling, Caleb screams.

Abigail sits up straight and wails, "what has happened to my baby? Bring me my baby!"

I go to pick the baby up and bring him to her. She sits up but is so weak that she drops him, to her lap.

"Lie down, lie down, Abigail, and put him against your side," I call.

My voice is so loud that Lydia and Phoebe come dashing into the kitchen. Pegg takes one look and knows Abigail is sick.

"Mistress Abigail is all right. I'm here. I'll take the baby when he finishes nursing," she says right beside Abigail's ear.

Lydia immediately asks, "Why is Mama's face so red?"

"She has a fever, child. Do not go too close to her, now. You might get sick."

Phoebe's eyes are like circles. Tears drip down her face. "Maman's going to die, I know it. I know it,"

"We will all take care of her. You help with Caleb," I say. "When the baby is settled down, I'll put him in your room. You can keep an eye on him."

"Mistress Rose, the kettle is boiling for the tea," Pegg says quietly. "I'll put the chamomile into hot water to set."

"Good, Pegg. That may help her sweat..." I jump up and go back to Abigail.

"I am so hot," Abigail murmurs. Pegg slides the baby away from her and carries him to the girls' bed to put him down.

Finally the tea is cool and we give it to Mistress. She sips some and then more and slides back to sleep. But in an hour, she is awake again. "I am burning, burning up," she wails. Pegg and I look at each other.

"Is very bad," Pegg says.

"Pegg, can you go and get a big pot of well water?" I ask.

"Is cold outside," she says.

"Hurry," I say. When she comes back, I have large linen clothes ready. One by one I soak them in the cold water, wring them out and place them on Abigail's body. She squirms and tries to get away, but I insist and lay them one after the other on her chest and back and stomach.

We work for an hour doing this. Finally, Abigail slips off to sleep, breathing more deeply. I put a hand on the side of her forehead as she rests. Her forehead is cooler.

"Let us let her be, now," I say.

Pegg and I light candles and sit up with her. When Abigail calls, I bring her Caleb to nurse. She cannot give much milk; her fever dries it up. Later, she calls again. I go to her, and her forehead is hot. We cannot go to the well now. It is dark... Pegg brings Abigail cold tea and sponges her with the water we have. I am so tired that I sleep on a blanket on the floor.

When the first light of dawn breaks through the windows, I hear her crying softly.

Her forehead burns. I get the last wet cloth.

"Rose, help me. I must get better," she says.

"I will help you, Mistress," I lay my hand on her shoulder. And then I lay down now with a sheep fleece over me on the floor. Pegg climbs up to the attic.

It is still very cold. The door opens.

"It is Sarah," Sarah whispers. She quickly closes the door and pulls me toward the fireplace away from the room where Abigail rests.

"It's time," Sarah says, "You must leave late today at dusk. The Bay may freeze. I can get Jacques from the barn at Nate's and get you both to Pierre and Marie Josèphe and the boat at Accabonac."

I close my eyes and a band of pain tightens my chest so that I cannot breathe. I pull Sarah down on the sheepskin beside me. We sit facing each other and Sarah's eyes gaze into mine. "Sarah, Mistress Abigail is sick, near sick unto death. And Nate," I turn away. "I cannot leave without seeing Nate again." My throat chokes up. I cannot speak.

Sarah's arms are around me. She holds me as she cries. "Dear friend, it will be worse for you, Rose, if you are alone here."

"Do not take Jacques, I beg you. I could not bear living here alone."

"But he will want... Pierre," Sarah says.

"I know, I know it is not fair to him. But please God, we will get away later."

"I cannot leave her. Go! I cannot bear it. Jonas is away. Abigail burns with fever. Go!"

"I must leave. The boat will not wait long," Sarah whispers. The door closes. I drop to my pallet my body and spirit limp. Through a dense wet mist in my head, I hear "Rose."

Mistress calls. I bring her cold tea. She still burns with fever. I change the baby's clothes and sink myself into caring for him.

CHAPTER THIRTY-THREE

NEWS FOR JONAS

The next morning, when I wake, cold morning light fills the room. It is late. Baby Caleb screams and Lydia pulls on my hand. Groggy, I stare up at her from the blanket on the floor where I have slept.

"Papa is back, Rose. He wants you outside."

Slowly it comes to me that Jonas may soon find out that Pierre and Marie Josèphe escaped from town last night. My hands tremble. Jonas will be angry, no doubt about that.

"How is your Maman?" I ask Lydia.

"She stood up, got a piece of bread to eat and sat down."

"She stood up?" I cannot believe it.

"Yes, she says she is still hot but feels better."

I stand up and pull Lydia's skinny body up to my chest and hug her. "Sweet Lydia, thank God your mom is feeling better. Run and call to your father that I will be out in a minute." I grab a shawl from the chair, slip my feet into moccasins and see that Abigail is nursing Caleb. Good! Her fever must have broken. Abigail nods at me, she must have heard Lydia, and I open the door to the yard. Jonas's wagon is there, filled with firewood. He busily unhitches Star and leads her to the barn. When, he sees me, he nods quickly and points at the wood. He must not know yet.

I drop the wagon's back, get a small cart to pile the logs in, and move them to the woodpile. When Jonas returns to the wagon, he does not say anything about his trip to New York City, whether he did get there, nor about Ephraim. But I don't think that I should ask.

Soon my hands are scratched from handling rough bark and my back aches from carrying the logs. But I work away, glad to be out of the house in the clear cold morning, and happy that Abigail can sit up and that her fever has dropped.

The sound of the sea rumbles in my ear. A steady northeast wind blows from the beach. The skin near the edges of my mouth cracks from the cold, Stray gulls plop down in the yard. A storm must be coming. The birds like to shelter inland away from the high winds and surf.

After a time, even though it is cold, sweat pours down my cheeks and soaks my undergarments. Jonas goes off to town. Months ago, he would not have left me alone outside. He would have worried about me trying to escape. Now, he will probably hear about the escape of Pierre and Marie Josèphe. I calm myself and tell myself that I can handle whatever happens.

Within a half-hour, he returns. I notice his half walk, half scrabble as he tries to rush towards me. He must have hurt his leg on his journey. I reach into the wagon bed to get a log and turn away from him. But he is too quick for me.

"Rose, Marie Josèphe, and your brother Pierre have fled from Amagansett. Did you know anything about this?" His voice is loud and challenging. He grips the side of the wagon and shakes it.

I try to distract him by dropping a big log with a loud thump, into my cart. Grabbing the cart's handle, I hold my breath and push hard to get the cart rolling, away from him and towards the house. Instead, he walks along beside me.

"Rose," he says slowly as if an idea is forming in his mind as he speaks, "Rose, Marie Josèphe was here only three days ago. You are a good friend of hers. She and Pierre escaped last night. Did she speak of this to you?"

Looking away and not answering the question, I say, "Master, Mistress was very sick last night, and she still has a fever."

"What about the baby?" He asks in a strangled voice.

"I think that the baby is well. I am not sure. His fever is gone."

Jonas forgets his question to me in his haste to get inside. He leaves me with the last logs in the wagon bed. I put them in the cart, drag them to the woodpile and pile them on top of the others.

Knowing it may be well to stay away from Jonas before he asks too many questions, I go to milk the cow who lows in the barn. When I finish milking, I carry the bucket inside.

Mistress sits in the one chair holding Caleb, and Master sits on the bench. They lean toward each other and speak so intently that I do not disturb them and tend to skim the cream from the milk.

Finally, Master realizes my presence, "Mistress Rose, we have had news of my son, Ephraim. In New York, I learned that he is alive, and has been ransomed by the French. He is on his way here, with two colonial soldiers to help him."

"Master, what good news!" I say. Even though I knew from Nate this might happen, I rejoice in my heart. He, I can see, is excited and nervous.

"Rose, you must do extra work to help me lay in more food for Ephraim. The French did not feed prisoners much. You must work for Mistress Mulford, taking care of her two babies. Master Mulford told me he would give me a good bushel of wheat for your services. Go now."

"I do not think that I should leave Mistress now, Master. I am happy to do the extra work. But Mistress is still weak and needs help."

"You are a bold girl to speak back to me." Master Jonas stares at me. "Do you forget your place?"

I open my mouth and clutch my fingers together in fright, but no words come out. Caleb smiles at me and coos, and suddenly Abigail speaks.

"Jonas, you don't know! She has cared for me through a bad fever. I need to have Rose here to nurse me back to strength." She stands and her voice is weak but steady. "I don't like to do it, but we can lease Pegg out for a few days to Mistress Mulford."

Abigail manages to hold her head up and look Jonas in the eye.

"If it were your son, you would do anything, anything," Jonas says to her. "You don't care about my child, my son. You never have."

"Jonas, let us not go over the old words again. Soon I will be strong and do everything I can to help Ephraim. You know that! You know that my heart is not closed upon your dear son. He is our son. But I must get strong. We must do as we can in this hard time."

"You may be sorry Abigail, for taking Rose's part. Soon she may flee like her brother and that Marie woman did last night!"

"What!" Abigail sits up, startled.

"Yes indeed. And I have few doubts that Rose did not know about it!" Jonas's voice rises and his face is red. "She will not tell me anything."

Abigail's eyes quickly seek mine. Again, she takes a deep breath, waits and asks me in a clear voice. "Rose, did you know that your family was to escape?"

Looking at her alone, I say, "I did."

"And why did you not go with them, then?"

"Mistress, I could not leave you alone and sick."

Abigail bows her head, and a tear slides down her cheek.

Jonas grunts. "If you are going to take care of her, Rose, get her some herb tea, woman." Then he says, "I will talk to Master Mulford about sending Pegg over to help out."

Mistress sinks back in her chair, "Please, Jonas, only let Pegg for a day. She is very helpful to us all here." She looks at me.

"I cannot tell you now, Rose, how thankful I am. But now, Rose, go into town and try to get apple juice for me. Take the girls, it will be good for them and you to get out of the house," Mistress says.

Lydia and Phoebe chatter and laugh and I have to warn them to dress warmly. I talk to Pegg about getting lunch for Mistress: a fish if we have one, and some late fall carrots and potatoes from the root cellar. "Be sure to add some thyme, "I remind her as my Maman would have told me.

The girls and I happily open the door, wave to Abigail, and leave. I carry a red clay jug for the cider, going from the North Village up the hill towards the village green. I do not dare to stop in Nate's workshop. We stop at a barn across the road from him. A neighbor drains pressed cider from a barrel into my jug. There is no sign of Nate. I cannot delay without reason. The girls walk scuffing the light cover of snow with their shoes.

"Is Mama well now?" Lydia asks.

"Mistress Woods died last week," Phoebe says, "And a baby in Montauk died last week as well."

As I turn to talk to Lydia, I notice that she is stretching out these days. She is near as tall as my shoulder and her lilac-blue eyes are often serious. She thinks now of more than dollies and skipping rope. It was the mother of her friend that died.

"I think she will be all right, Lydia. Your Mama did have a dangerous fever last night. But she seems better today. I will ask the herb lady to stop by and give her a tonic."

Before I can turn around, Sarah's familiar voice strikes my ear. "G'day, Rose, here is a watch for you to take to Nate to fix," she says loudly. "I am in a big hurry. Could you help me out?"

She whispers, "Nate waits in that small shed to tell you of what happened last night. I will take the girls to see my aunties' new ducks." The girls run away along with Sarah.

My heart pounds as I walk down the narrow path to the little barn. Nate quietly opens the door. Our eyes meet.

"I believe they are safe in Guilford," he says. "And Jacques lives with me still."

CHAPTER THIRTY-FOUR

THE STRANGER

Winter days are short, and we save our candles, so we work less. I have time to think. Because I stayed and helped her, Mistress Abigail grows stronger. I am glad that I may have saved her life. Now I think my mind and heart will be clear when it comes time for me to try to leave here, if I leave here.

Lydia and Phoebe beg me to tell a story, to pass the time. But just as I am racking my brain to create a tale from Acadia, Temperance knocks and rushes into the room. "Half the town is talking, there is a stranger down by the pond," she says.

"Tell us what is happening. We were just asking Rose for a story," Lydia says.

"The stranger speaks gibberish. He hides his head in his arms and no-one can make him talk straight," Temperance says.

"Let us go see, Mama," Lydia begs. "It is so dull just to sit here and look at the fire."

A smile brightens Abigail's face, "It is dull, just to sit here with all of us?" she asks with a chuckle. "All right, Lydia, you may go with Rose, but be sure to stay well back from this person." She turns to me, "Rose, I'm sure the men will watch this stranger but be careful."

"Yes, Mistress." Like Lydia, I am glad to get out of the house. Phoebe protests that she wants to come with us, also, but Mistress says no, it might frighten her, so Phoebe stomps out of the room and looks about for Pegg.

Temperance, Lydia and I start on our way, chattering back and forth and a little bit scared about what lies ahead. A light rain sprinkles our faces but it is not enough to stop us. We pass Nate's workshop. Mist hangs over the trees and the buildings on Main Street. The bell tolls the fourth hour... A cluster of burning torches glows through the fog near the pond. As we get closer to the crowd and the torches, Lydia clutches my hand tightly.

Twenty people sparsely gather in a circle around a person seated on a tree trunk. We walk up to the group and stand well behind the people. I hold one of Lydia's hands and Temperance has the other.

There, in front of us, is a short, stocky man. He wears woolen trousers, ripped at one knee and a coat stitched together from leather skins. His hat droops over his face and beard. As we come closer, he shakes his head back and forth mumbling words that sound like French.

One man calls out, "Get him to talk straight, or we'll put him in the stocks for the night. He may be a spy." "I think that he speaks French," the blacksmith's wife says. "Is there anyone here speaks that tongue?"

I hold Lydia's hand tightly and say nothing. The person beside me turns slightly. Her face is inches from mine. "Rose is here," she calls.

"Bring her up!" calls the watchman.

Temperance puts her arm around Lydia's shoulder and puts the other arm around my shoulder for an instant. "I'll be here," she says.

As I walk forward, I see the man shiver. When I stand in front of him, he drops his head so that his hat blocks my view of his face. I crouch down to better see him but do not go too close.

"*Du pain!*" he mutters. "*J'ai faim!*"

Someone hands me a loaf of bread. I hold it in front of him. One of the stranger's hands shoots out grabs the loaf, tears it in half and stuffs the food in his mouth. Crumbs hang on his blond beard. He stomps a foot and cries, "*Encore!*"

"Tell us who you are," a harsh voice behind me calls.

I ignore the villager's rough words. This man speaks French, and I wonder about him. I try to think of a calming word to say. "Look at me stranger," I say gently to him in French. The stranger lifts his eyes to mine. But he seems shocked out of his own mind and living in a half French, half English world. It is good that I can speak in both his worlds.

The appearance of his strong square jaw, and the look in his brown eyes, startles me. He looks a bit like Jonas. Could it be that this is his son, Ephraim? I move backwards, shocked. "You will not be hurt," I say to him in French, "but speak in English if you can. People want to know who you are and why you are here."

Extending one arm towards me, he rests it lightly on my knee. His eyes dart back and forth. The villagers press close around us.

My mind and heart flashback to the day I was brought here. Villagers crowded around me. They told me not to speak French. Now, I am one of the villagers, at least by place.

With the thought in my head that this may be Ephraim, Jonas's son, I ask, "What is your name?"

This man laces his fingers over his eyes. He drops his head, and sits cross-legged like a child, and he does not speak.

"Hold on," the watchman calls out, "there is a man with a rifle running down the road towards us. "Take care, take care."

The soldier calls out. "He got away from us!" The soldier's leg is bandaged, and he runs with a tilting step. His face is thin and hungry-looking, and he wears the well-worn uniform of the colonial militia. Breathing heavily, the soldier stops beside us.

"What are you talking about? Who got away from you? Are you looking for this person?" the watchman asks, pointing at the ragged stranger.

The soldier pauses as he had been breathing hard. He peers under the floppy leather hat of the stranger. "Yes, this is the man I escorted. I was bringing him here. As we were walking down the road past Southampton, especially after passing through Bridgehampton, he started to point at houses and mumble. Then he dashed away into the trees and left us behind. His name is Ephraim." The soldier stops and takes a deep breath.

A gasp of "Oh!" escapes from the people behind me. "It must be Jonas's son!" a lady calls. "I will run and find Jonas," our neighbor says.

So my guess is right. I hear people crying, and I am sure this is Ephraim. I feel tears streaming down my own face. But I stay beside Ephraim, and say in French, as that seems to be the language to which he answers, "Ephraim, you are home. You are home!"

I hear more people behind me saying, "He's here, let him through, show him!"

I turn and see Master Jonas running towards us. Putting my hand up high, and waving, I call, "Master! He is here!"

Master Jonas rushes up beside me, and then pulls his son gently off the ground. "Ephraim, Ephraim," he says. His face is wet with tears. "My son, my son, you are home."

Ephraim pulls back and shakes his head. "No," he says.

Jonas tries to put his arms around Ephraim. But Ephraim ignores him, jerks his arm away. Tears stream down Jonas's face as he talks to the soldier who has just run up to us. "What is wrong with my son? Tell me. He was born in this village. Now, he seems like another person, but it is he. What has happened? For God's sake, tell me," he shouts at the man.

"Steady man, steady. These things sometimes happen to young soldiers who cannot bear the horror of the blood, the killing, the torture," the man says.

"Master, someone's brought a bench, you can sit here," I say to him. The man goes on speaking to Jonas, "We were just able to put together what might have happened to him. As you can see, he does not understand much and seems to speak mostly in simple French. We think he was shot in a battle near Oswego. Under his hat, you can see that he has had a head wound. We know he was a prisoner of war in Montreal and the regular French guards treated him well. Perhaps the wound and the captivity affected his mind. Now, he speaks only a few words: mixed French and English," the soldier tells Jonas.

Jonas puts a handout to Ephraim again, but Ephraim slaps it away. The villagers now drift away. A hum of words floats back to my ears. "Ephraim," "so strange now," "what could have happened to him?"

Temperance catches my eye and I nod my head towards Mistress Abigail's. She and Lydia walk away, but I see Lydia's face as she turns back to see what is happening.

Ephraim doesn't seem to understand what his former guard says about him. He just wants food. He jostles me as he reaches for food.

Jonas tries again to talk to the boy. But Ephraim crazily shakes his head in a crazy way. "Food?" he says to me in French again. "*Du pain*," he begs. Ephraim puts his hands to his mouth and pretends as if he was eating. He pulls me away from Master Jonas.

Jonas stands with his arms dropped to his sides. His rugged strong face with a firm jaw, sags like a sack. "Lead him home, Rose," Jonas mutters in a sad voice. "He can eat at home. He will not come with me. He cannot speak to me, my own son. I do not know if he even knows me."

"Yes, Master," I say. I speak a few words in French to Ephraim. "Viens-come," "Pain-bread," and like a four-year-old, Ephraim trustfully takes my hand.

Jonas shakes his head, and tears well into his eyes again. "Go with Rose, Ephraim," he says. But he does not lay a hand on him. Jonas starts walking home. Ephraim and I follow him. Ephraim holds my hand. Moonlight lights our path on the ground. When we enter the house, Mistress Abigail sits in a chair holding baby Caleb and stares at Ephraim. Then she looks at my hand holding Ephraim's.

"He looks so different," she says uncertainly.

"Abigail, the boy is sick," Jonas whispers. "He will not come near me, but he follows Rose like a dog."

"He is wounded," she says, quickly laying Caleb in his cradle.

"I am not sure of that," Jonas says. "But he is mixed up in his head. He can say a few words and seems only to understand Rose when she speaks in French."

"I do not know what is wrong with him, Mistress," I say. "He seems to know some French words and some English words. I do know that he is hungry."

Abigail quickly gets up and slices some fresh bread from a warm loaf on the trivet and gets some cheese. She ladles samp into a big black pot and warms it. When Ephraim slurps down the warm cornmeal samp, for the first time, he smiles. "Is samp," he says.

I smile in agreement and nod at him. And the memory of my first time in this kitchen returns: I was starving, and I was given little. He gets two bowls more.

Master Jonas has made a bed with quilts near the fire and settled himself into a chair. "Sleep, Ephraim," he says. Jonas points to the quilts. And he looks at me to speak to his son.

"*Dormez bien*, Ephraim," I say. I watch the boy as I edge to the ladder to the attic. Ephraim starts to follow me but Jonas gently leads him back to the quilts. Ephraim lies down near the warm fire, as I go up the stairs to the freezing attic.

I feel so alone now that Pierre and Marie Josèphe have left. This night, I wish that I could leave tomorrow to join them. But only I can help Ephraim.

CHAPTER THIRTY-FIVE

NATE COMES

As winter passes, Ephraim relaxes. He sleeps on his own in the lean-to. He goes with Jonas in the wagon and follows his simple commands. He feels comfortable with his father now. But their relationship will never be the same. Jonas accepts that now. Jonas is nearly called up to fight the French who are attacking English forts upstate. But he is able to talk his way out of service because of Ephraim.

Ephraim eats and eats. That keeps Pegg and me busy, but I feel free of the responsibility of translating for Ephraim now. He has regained some of the English he knew before he was wounded.

And so, I have time to think of the Acadians in Guilford, across the Bay from East Hampton. Ephraim is steady now and Mistress Abigail, back to her old self and able to handle the larger family she has now. Lydia helps her and before long Phoebe will also. They could live without me. But I still am a prisoner here. I cannot walk away and climb on a boat to Connecticut.

Snow falls heavily on some days, soft, and a delight to the children of the village. When they get away from their chores, they steal a few minutes to make snowballs and snowmen. But when snow falls so thick and heavy that it coats my face with flakes and so deep that I have to jump like a leapfrog until I shovel a path, it is a problem for me.

Weather like this reminds me of what used to be my home, Acadia. I have the ocean here, as I did there, but we don't have the lovely river here. On the Annapolis River, we could canoe for miles and in the winter, we could skate for miles.

One day, when I manage to slog through the drifts to the barn to milk, Nate comes. Master had asked him to bring in extra hay for the cow. I have been thinking of him so much, wavering back and forth, should I accept his lovely offer to stay with him, or should I hope to get away from here and try to travel to Guilford?

As I straighten up from milking, I see Nate leaning on the stall partition facing me. He has been watching me, I sense. But now, his face is still and his eyes downcast as if he is thinking. His brown hair still has a few flakes of snow, his cheeks are ruddy from the cold and his arm and hand hang over the stall side, as he is deep in thought. I notice his broad strong hand, but the skin has deep cracks from the cold. I look at him for a moment before he lifts his eyes. Our eyes meet, and as they do, I felt a deep peace settle into my heart. And then a quick ripping pain. How can I leave him? Such a good man.

"How are things going with Ephraim?" he asks quietly.

I look at him. We are alone here at least for the moment. "It is hard for him. I do not know sometimes how to help him as I did not know him before. But he is more with Jonas now."

"You, Rose, help everyone," Nate says with a half-smile. "It is so strange that you were dragged here from your own land, against your will and yet you help those in need."

"It is what my Maman and Papa and the others did. It is in my blood and heart, I guess." We look at each other, a long look on my part and worried, on his.

"Will you ever love anyone, Rose, deeply love and commit yourself to a man? Is it in your spirit to do that, Rose?" Although quiet, his deep voice rasps with frustration.

"I loved in a young way, Nate, once, I told you. Is André dead or alive? I don't know. He was put on a different ship from me, Until I am sure that he is gone, dead, married perhaps, I cannot give myself to another." I look at him, "that is what love is, isn't it? Giving oneself?"

"It is, Rose," his voice breaks and I come out of the stall and fall into his arms.

"Nate, Nate, I am so sorry."

He gently holds me as he straightens up. "Never forget how I love you, Rose. If life goes wrong for you, never forget, once, how deeply you were loved."

I cannot speak. Nate opens his arms, and then he holds me. Then, he wipes the tears from my cheeks as gently as if those big hands were picking violets in springtime.

"I must go into this blasted blizzard and help out at home… Do you need help with the milk bucket?"

"Just to the house door," I say. He takes the bucket and strides out into the swirling snowflakes, and I wipe my smelly hand on my wool skirt to clean the milk from it.

This is moment I will relive for all my life. We have parted. We will see each other again I know, but our ways will be different now. I sigh and my spirits sink so low that I do not answer even sweet Phoebe who calls plaintively from the door of the kitchen for me to come in and help her churn the cream.

In the kitchen, Jonas teaches Ephraim how to use a small hand-held loom. The girls, Lydia and Phoebe, watch, puzzled that a grown man like Ephraim cannot quickly master a task they do without looking at their fingers.

The winter days pass slowly as they always seem to when it is hard to move about because of the snow and rain. Gradually the air grows lighter, rid of the heavy dampness of winter. Light breezes blow first the stink of cow manure and rotted corn stalks as they are spread on the fields, then the sweet freshness of apple blossoms.

Ephraim now goes willingly with Jonas. He is not to my knowledge a whole man, but he seems to be happy, and Jonas gradually resigns himself to live with the Ephraim he has now.

Before we know it, cherry-picking time is here, and after the busy days of picking, sorting, and cooking berries, the last day is a holiday, something I have never seen or dreamed about in this somber town. We young people get to visit, and everyone gobbles gobs of cherries with mounds of whipped cream. Thanks to Abigail's words, I am allowed to go to it all. Sarah is here, and Nate, and Temperance and I feel very at home in this place. It is the first time since I came here that the village life seems like my old Acadian life.

I begin to open the garden for Mistress Abigail and see that the willow shoot I brought from Annapolis Royal has rooted in the moist soil at the back, near the stream. Life goes on. The willow thrives here, transplanted to new soil but still it has sunk new roots. Yet, I do not feel that this is my growing land.

CHAPTER THIRTY-SIX

SHOCKING NEWS

I hear Jonas's voice calling, "Rose," one morning several more weeks after cherry-picking time. When I look up, I see a small flock of ewes moving down the road towards Amagansett under the care of a young shepherd. A lone hawk dives to attack a scrawny ewe in his talons but the boy scares him off, although the sheep scatter, baaing wildly. Jonas stands for a moment. "I love to see the sheep taken off to new grazing plots in Montauk. It means that summer is here."

He looks at me. "Ephraim is so different. First, he was different and now," we look at each other, "he is not the person he was."

"I know what you say, Master, but isn't he happy in his own way, now?"

"He is Rose. This morning he works for a bayman, lifting his fish traps and digging for clams. I think he will grow into a good bayman's helper… doesn't have to talk much, out on the water… He loves it."

Jonas looks as happy as I have ever seen him look. His face has just a few wrinkles near his brown eyes. His glance is open, his voice steady,

"Rose, step over here under this elm tree. You may feel faint if you are in the sun."

I do as he says, puzzled.

"Rose, I have just learned that all Acadians in New York State have been freed from bondage by the governor." Jonas for the first time, puts a gentle hand on my shoulder. "The East Hampton Town Council has given me money to pay for you and Jacques to travel to Guilford, to meet there with your family, if that is where you want to go."

I do stagger, and he holds my arm for a moment. My heart so soars with joy that it is with an effort that I stop from falling to my knees in prayer to the Lord.

Jonas looks at me kindly and with the direct look of an equal. "Rose, my family will ask you to help perhaps for a week and then help you prepare to leave. Abigail and the girls will be very sad. Again he looks directly at me, "I understand what you did for Abigail at the birth of Caleb and this winter in helping her recover. You helped her in body and spirit and more than that, you brought my son, Ephraim, back from the hells of war."

We are at the gate of his house as he smiles slowly as he so often did in the past, but this time with a glint of humor in his eye. "Now, you have not left yet, so you'd best be busy and help Pegg in the garden."

"I will, Master… And Master?"

"Don't test me, Rose," he says with a hint of impatience.

"Please be good to Pegg, Master."

"Ah, Rose. We will be good to her. We hope to free her when she can take care of herself and move away if she wishes…" He butts into himself. "But I do not want to tell her, now."

"So, in a week, Rose, you will leave here," He looks closely at me, "If you and Nate wish it so, you both will leave here, together."

I look at Master freely, not cowering as I might have in the past. "Master Jonas, thank you for this news. I need time now to walk and think. Tell the others I will be with them soon, But I must… walk and think." And so, I do.

Long ago, in Acadia, André pressed a tiny wooden bird that he had carved for me into my hand. The tiny bird, made of pine, has half-spread wings as if the bird is ready to fly. For a year now, that little bird has lived in my dark pocket, with little hope of air or flight. Now, I am leaving this place, East Hampton. The little bird may fly again, but where?

How hard it has been to work here as a servant, fearfully answering Jonas, 'Yes, Master' to all his commands. His hawk eyes spurred me to wear a dripping wet chemise, wrestle with sheep, work in the garden until after nightfall, carry wood until my back ached... On top of that, carrying slops to the pigs, dragging their waste into baskets, and spreading it on the vegetable garden. And then my usual task of milking, spinning, cooling, butchering tasks, and every day, without fail, mashing corn into samp in the pestle and a hundred other chores as well. Yet now I see that much of the work was just about what Mistress had done if she was stronger.

True, that night in the stocks nearly broke my spirit, but all these things did not break me. Not even when Jonas stood back when the Acadian travelers appeared on our beach and let them be taken under guard to New York City and even threatened me with the same fate...

That there are people like him in the world, I did not know this when I was young in Acadia. I know now. Jonas has changed some, now. But I am glad to leave him forever.

I am not glad to leave everyone in this village. But for him, yes!

Like a frantic bird trapped in a snare, I have the feeling that I must get away to fly. Whether that is true, I'm not sure. Too long have we been prisoners of the English colonists here. Now, all the Acadians in New York are free to leave. But England has stolen our home, Acadia. I can fly... But where...?

CHAPTER THIRTY-SEVEN

ONWARD

Pegg learned last night that I am free to leave East Hampton. At the well, she hardly lifted her eyes to me when she said, "Goodbye, Rose." I know now that her black skin traps her here inside a birdcage where she is free to move around, but she just beats herself against the wires if she wishes to leave.

At the well, I took her hand, hugged her. "Goodbye," I said to this woman who gave me her food, her blanket, and her courage. Pegg turns from me without a word and lugs the heavy water bucket back inside. Her wings may never open. My heart breaks.

And now, on my last day, I must say goodbye to broad-shouldered Nate who returns Jacques to me. Nate taught me much about what true love is. Our hearts are joined forever.

"When will we leave Rose? Where will we go?" Jacques chatters. And then he remembers Nate. He turns to the big man and clutches him around his legs, crying.

"I brought you tools, little brother. See a small hammer for your small hands and a small chisel. And see, a little leather case for you to keep them in." Nate bends way down to give the present to Jacques, who is struck silent.

"Nate, Nate," I say and find myself putting my hands into his huge ones. He holds them tightly. My eyes fill with tears. This good, good man. Life is full of twists and turns. He suffers for my leaving. I do not know what is ahead. Yet, he lets me go. Just barely.

"I will wait to hear from you, dear one," he says quietly.

He gently tips my chin up to look into my eyes and puts his arms around me once more. His arms, the security of them, is with me just for an instant.

"Nate, I cannot say goodbye. I have to go and see my people. I will come back or, I will send word that I go on with them. Can you wait, will you wait?"

There are people about. His eyes are wet. He takes my hand in between his warm, rough ones, presses them together for an instant. "Yes, I will," he says.

And with a quick grin, he throws a comment over his shoulder. "But not forever." Then, he turns and walks down the road in his own way, his stride long and loose.

Temperance rushes up with a cloth-covered basket. "I cannot believe you are leaving. It feels like you have been here forever. I will miss you whatever will Sarah do with you gone." She is crying but she thrusts a cloth-covered basket into my arms. "Godspeed," she says and runs off, shaking her head.

Mistress Abigail has been standing by the gate. She calls and Phoebe and Lydia rush out to me while Caleb runs to play in a mud puddle.

"Will we ever see you again, Rose?" Phoebe asks, her freckled face serious.

"There is a chance that you may, Phoebe," I look at her and grab her hand, "Love every day and don't light candles in the hay barn! I wish so much that I can come back and see you all grown up."

Lydia, listening, bounces back and forth on her two feet. She looks bored with the serious things I've said to Phoebe. Finally, Lydia bursts out, "Rose, someday, I will come to you! Wait and see!" Then she runs to haul Caleb out of the mud puddles and bring him to Abigail.

"And someday, she may," Mistress Abigail says. "She has the spirit and the courage." Looking at Caleb,

Mistress Abigail says, "Know you have a little cousin here, Rose." I look to her, and she pauses, "I cannot say so many things in my heart, so I will just say, 'Thank you. Thank you for everything and Godspeed."

I look around for Jonas. He leans against the house wall at the front door. Girding my courage, I walk over to him.

"Goodbye, Jonas," I say, accentuating his name. He stares at the ground, looks up finally, says, "Goodbye," and turns to walk into the house. He turns back, "Thank you," he says, "for what you've done for Abigail and Ephraim." And he walks in the door without looking back.

A fisherman from Accabonac drives a rattling cart into the yard and swings my battered little trunk and my sac with my cooking pot into the back. He covers it with an old blanket Abigail has given me. Jacques climbs in with his things.

Silently, villagers watch us leave as the cart turns right out of the yard and travels down a dirt path on a soft spring day with birds flitting in and out of the bushes.

I put my hand into my pocket and feel my little bird and say to myself, "Little one, we are flying to find a home. I do not know where yet."

The man drives onto the road to Accabonac. "You go home?" The fisherman asks softly.

"Truly, I do not know. I no longer have a home," I tell him. He turns towards me, his tanned, weather-beaten face filled with concern. "You'll find one, girlie. You've got guts and heart," he says. I clutch the silver pieces in my hand that Abigail gave me from the whale bounty. And suddenly my spirit soars. God bless Mistress Abigail and keep her. But I am on my way to my beloved Acadians. I may soon be with Pierre and Marie Josèphe, perhaps my Maman and André, and who knows who else. And Jacques is with me.

When we reach the beach at Accabonac, Sarah and her father are there, waiting. Sarah is crying. She hands me a basket, "For your journey," she whispers. "Oh, Rose..."

"Thank you, thank you. You gave me my heart back." I tell her and stop, overcome.

"Try to send us word," The schoolmaster Master Wells says.

"Yes, Master. I'll try. But know, without you, my heart would have broken. *Merci, mon ami.*"

Offshore, a sloop sways in the waves, its sails flapping. "Be quick. The tide is changing," the boatman's helper calls. Jacques and I wade out to the dory. The man hauls Jacques aboard and I clamber in like an old lady. The fisherman grabs the oars and pulls deep. The boat scrapes on gravel and lurches to a stop.

"Out!" the man pokes Jacques. Jacques jumps onto the gravel bar and pushes, but it is not enough. The man jumps out, gets behind the dory and pushes, to clear the gravel bar. He clambers back in again and pulls Jacques aboard. The boat is free from the bar. A soft breeze ruffles the waters of the bay. He rows us out to the sloop. We board, the sloop tacks for the harbor entrance. And we are away.

CHAPTER THIRTY-EIGHT

GUILFORD

We land at New London after a calm sail across Bay waters. I thank and pay the boatman and we walk off the pier and see houses and wagons nearby. Using some more of my money from the whale sighting, I speak to a driver who tells me, "twill be an overnight journey to Guilford." He will take us for a fee, and I pay him.

After a night's stay in a travelers' hut, we go on and finally reach Guilford.

Jacques bursts out, "Where is Pierre? Is he here, Rose? Where is Marie?" The wagon jolts to a stop. We are in front of a sizeable inn-like building where people hurry about, as if this is a regular welcome place for travelers. Another passenger in the wagon asks the driver if this is Guilford and the driver nods yes.

Jacques who is sitting close beside me, has been silent. He suddenly says, "Where are they?"

"They didn't know that we were coming, Jacques. We'll find them. Don't worry. Come, we'll climb down and pick up our things from the back of the wagon. I can find someone to help us."

After our things are unloaded, down the street comes a woman whom I ask, in English, "Are there Acadians near here?" She peers at me.

"Why do you ask?" she asks.

"I look for my brother," I say.

Her look softens. "Over this way. I'll show you. My son has his cart here and can take you to where the Acadians stay."

She smiles at Jacques. "Your name, son?"

"Jacques, ah, James," he says, stumbling over his words.

"Such a bad time you people have had," the woman shakes her head. She turns to me, "Your people live near The Acadian House. It is just down the street. We will drop you there."

I do not speak to her as the wagon passes slowly under the trees. I cannot talk. My heart surges with hope: maybe we will see Maman and Madeleine. Oh, I hope it is so. Beads of sweat drip into my eyes and as I rub my eyes, my hand trembles. What joy it would be to feel my mother's strong arms around me, look deep into her hazel eyes and hear her rich, rollicking laugh. And how much I wish to find Madeleine, sweet frail child, to swing her round me like a whirly wheel, and hear her laugh, sweet and clear.

How will it be to meet Andre? if he is here. Is he the same? Am I the same? Is the bond between us strong and unbroken like two vines grown together over the years.? Or is one or both of the vines withered, or is each growing strong and green, alone.

I must go on. I came here to Guilford for this moment. Hope and fear jostle around in my heart until I am almost sick.

In a while, we are in front of a large two-story house with neatly spaced windows and a sloping shingled roof. In front of the house, an older woman sits slumped over a bench with a little girl beside her. Both are shelling peas. The woman sits up and waves and my heart jumps, could this be? She calls out, in French, "Good day... Who seek you?"

In a shaking voice in French, I say, "I am Rose, an Acadian girl from Belle Isle. I look for Pierre and Marie Josèphe, and..." my voice quavers. Jacques runs over to the lady. "We look for our Maman, Cécile, and my little sister, Madeleine."

The woman's dark eyes seek out mine. Her face is like stone. Speaking in French, she says, "You must be Rose, Pierre's sister. *C'est vrai?*" she adds.

"*Oui, madame.* It is true." I again look at her and those sad dark eyes hold mine.

"Your mother and your sister, I do not know. But Marie Josèphe is here, now, in the garden." She points to the side of the house where a large garden, fenced with grapevines, thrives." Marie Josèphe took over the running of the garden, and she works there every day. Boy," she says, looking at Jacques, "run back there and see if you find her."

"Oh!"

I hear Marie Josèphe's familiar shriek, "Jacques!" and I have to smile. Marie Josèphe, considerably stouter than she used to be, rushes out of the little garden hut.

"Thank God!" she calls and runs to meet me. "Thank God you are here. We leave for Acadia next week. Oh my god, there is so much…" she falls into my arms, steps back and looks for Jacques. Warily, he steps away, and she just catches the side of his face with a kiss.

"Jacques. Jacques. In these few months, you've grown tall. Pierre will not believe it."

"When will I see him?" Jacques demands.

"Tonight, tonight. At sundown, he will return from the fishing boat and tonight, we will sup together. *C'est bien?*"

"It is good," Jacques says quietly but with a big smile on his face.

Several people pour out of the Acadian House. They are dressed in the familiar Acadian way. But their clothes, especially the women's striped skirts, are worn and faded, and the men's clothes are ragged and patched.

It is as though I am living in a dream to see Acadians, many of them thin and pale, who have lived through the bad times. They are fortunate to live together and the citizens of Guilford, Connecticut have given them their own house to live in. But times have been hard for them, it seems. My breath catches in my throat as I hear Acadians, young and old, speaking Acadian French. "Is that Rose from Belle Isle, could it be?" I hear in a variety of voices in both French and English. Then, an old friend from Annapolis Royal stands in front of me and stares at me. "How are you?" he probes.

"I am well, now," I say. "But it has been so hard. We have lost so many."

All through the afternoon, I visit with Acadians from Annapolis Royal, from farms near my hamlet, and other places in Acadia. With deep sadness in my heart, I hear their stories: removal from Acadia on the English ships, wives swept overboard, children lost to smallpox, the hardships of their first days in Connecticut, and then, I look up.

There is Pierre.

My heart drops. He towers over me. He is more solid now. Good food must have filled him out from the build of youth to the size of a grown man. His size scares me for I still fear talking with him on serious matters. Because I am younger, he has a way of giving orders and not listening to me.

A flying body sails past me and into Pierre's arms. Jacques of course. Over Jacques's shoulder, we look at each other and in the look are memories of past days with our family. Pierre's face floats in the middle of memories of Maman, Papa and Madeleine and then, the memory of André. And so, I burst out their names; "André, Maman, Madeleine?"

The pool of sorrow in Pierre's eyes is so deep that I gasp and fall to the ground.

I wake with Pierre's arm around my shoulder and a sturdy Acadian woman by my side. Jacques is crying, so I reach out to him. He may not know what has caused me to faint. "I am all right, Jacques. Don't worry. Please get me some food," I say as I get up from the ground.

And while Jacques rushes off, Pierre says in a low voice. "Rose, our dear Maman is gone."

I clutch his arm for fear that I will faint again. "No," I moan. For her to die in captivity, my sweet, beautiful Maman. "Oh my God!"

Solid Pierre's eyes brim with tears, too. "Rose, never have I felt so bitter a pain as when I heard this. And we are not alone, hundreds of Acadian families suffered like this. Thousands maybe…"

"André was on the ship with them. Is he…?"

"He is alive and has kept Madeleine with him…. It is best that you hear the story from him."

"Where is André, and when can I see him?" my words fly out of my mouth.

"Later. He will come by with fish he begs for at the New London wharves."

"Oh my god, there is so much, to uncover from the past. But this is why I came; I have to know."

"He will want to tell you himself," Pierre says calmly.

We walk together to sit on a bench under a tree. Pierre puts an arm around my shoulder as we talk with Marie Josèphe and the others. Evening draws on and the families gather nearby on the grass. In Acadia, the women might have brought spinning wheels, but here they sew, as they have no flocks of sheep to give them wool. The young boys play ball and Jacques quickly makes friends, speaking French and joining the game.

It is good to be with my people again. I fall into the old ways of listening to them, to hear and remember their wisdom. We don't have much to eat but we fill our hearts with talk and singing songs and hymns.

As the day fades, Pierre says, "André usually comes about this time." His eyes have a question in them that goes unasked. I gather myself, stand up and smooth my skirt, straighten my cap and walk over and talk to the others, keeping an eye out for André.

Will I know him? I think so, but beyond that, all I can do is wait. I nibble bread and cheese. When I hear a wagon coming, I look up to see if it is he. Several wagons continue past me down the road.

Then a wagon comes down the road from town as we did, turns into the road in front of Acadian House, and goes to the side of the house. In a minute, I see a man hoisting baskets and easily unloading them from his wagon. When he is finished, he hitches the horse to a post and walks towards the group I am in. My heart jolts, could it be?

I look and look. The man throws his head back to shake the shaggy hair out of his eyes and looks over at us all.

"The captains were generous today. Baskets of sole and even one of coquilles," he calls. "There they are," he turns and points at the baskets.

"Now, how about a quick beer?" The voice is deep with a touch of fun, and I am not sure I know it. He is about twenty yards away. But when my eyes link with his eyes, I know, I know. "André!" I call before I can stop myself.

He stops and stares and takes one more step forward. "Rose!" he cries out. And there is a murmur around me as he walks quickly towards me. I walk away from the other people to meet him, and we stand together, where he stops, just at the side of the house, under a big tree. I stand, looking at him, not knowing what to do or say. But Jacques has no such problem. He rushes up to our old friend. "I am Jacques. I am eight years old now, André do you still have a gun?"

"*Incroyable*! Unbelievable, Rose," André calls to me over Jacques's head. When he releases Jacques from a bear hug, he opens his arms and crushes me lightly against his chest, puts his hands on my shoulders, and then lightly steps back. "So much, so much for us to say."

"Did you catch that fish yourself?" Jacques insists on knowing.

André puts a hand to his ear, "My friend, *parlez-vous français*?"

"*Un peu*," Jacques says, looking at the ground.

"Ah, already we know our loss, eh Rose?"

"It will come back to him in Acadie," I say in French.

"How lovely it is to hear your voice, richer now, but still speaking the tongue of your youth. They did not take that away, at least!" André grips my hand again.

The need for news about dear Maman and Madeleine fills my heart now, and the words tumble out. I cannot hold them back, "Tell me the news about Maman and Madeleine."

"My Rose," André says, taking my hand and holding it gently, glancing at Jacques, "I will tell you of it later. Not now."

I stagger as my head spins with buried feelings. Jacques looks at me anxiously.

"I'm all right, don't worry, Jacques."

I whisper to André. "Later, you must tell me more."

"I will. Here, sit for a moment and rest."

As I sit across from him on a bench, he takes my hand. "Rose, I have so much to say but I want to wait until just we two are together. We can talk later this evening."

I wonder at his calmness when my feelings are rising and falling like storm waves. I could not speak now if wished to. But Jacques of course can and chatters away in French to André. He shows him his new set of tools and tells him that he can now, nearly, make a chair. He is still talking as we walk back together to the group.

"André, do you wish to join us tonight?" one of the older men asks.

"With Rose's consent, she and I may take a ride to the beach later... We have much to talk about," André says, and I nod.

CHAPTER THIRTY-NINE

THE ENGLISH AGAIN

As he drives away, a few heads turn and look at him and me, but then the talking goes on as to what we Acadians should do.

One woman, a sturdy petite old lady, *ancienne*, says, "Soon we all will be free. Even though I am old, I vote to go back to whatever we find in Acadie."

She reminds me of my tiny, grand-mère but of course it is not her. Pierre has said that my me-mere most probably died on the ship she was loaded on in Grand Pre. Another wave of grief sweeps over me and I look down at the ground, without words.

Pierre steps beside the old woman. "I go to Canada, to Acadie, if I can, and I cast my vote to take this grand-mère with us. No one else can have her!" he says. It is good that Pierre lightens our hearts with his bold talk. A chuckle tickles my ribs as others join in the laughter. It is right, so. We Acadians stick with each other. We will help each other.

Some like Pierre hope to go back to Canada, some to an island owned by France, Saint Pierre -Miquelon, off the coast of Newfoundland. The man who sailed me here said he had heard that in New York City, Acadians were given passage to the French island of Martinique.

Just before we left East Hampton, Abigail had read in Le Journal, that the English government now ruled that all Acadians had to be out of English province within nineteen months of the end of the War. But I didn't believe her. How could that be?

It has come to me now, that, had Nate and I made promises, we would have had to travel, I don't know where, to live together. For now, with this new English rule, I could not have lived on English soil. Certainly, not in East Hampton.

People here tell me that Acadians from New York are now being urged to settle in the French Antilles. Such treachery: the English do not trust us still, to live free in their colonies. They still give orders about what to do and where to move.

The happier news I heard was that it seems like the province of Louisiane, at the end of the great river, has many Acadians and is open to more settlers.

Pierre continues to speak of going back to Acadie. I look at Pierre, I realize how much he looks like Papa when Papa was young and strong, and I toddled after him.

Pierre has Papa's tousled black hair, his open, friendly face, a sturdy strong body with muscled arms, but different from him, he has a bowlegged gait. Pierre now works so many fishing ships that his gait has gotten to match the sea. Still, Pierre has Papa's boisterous manner as well, a gift that I do not have.

"I plan to start for Acadia next week," Pierre says as he looks at Marie Josèphe's big belly, "Now that we are man and wife and we have a little one on the way, we want to get there before the ice and cold set in." He looks at Jacques. "I hope that my brother Jacques will come with me."

Jacques rushes forward and stands proudly beside him.

The little group looks at me and then is distracted. André has returned and drives up in his wagon, in front of the group.

"Stay! André," a genial voice calls. "We sing tonight, later, and we need you."

André smiles. "*Non, mes frères*. With Pierre's permission, Rose and I will share a visit to the beach just now." People look at each other and even Pierre seems uneasy about André's words. But as I have already agreed to go with him, I smile at them all and climb into his wagon, leaving them as I glance back, gazing after us with surprised faces.

CHAPTER FORTY

TOGETHER ALONE

André drives away from the Acadian House and finally stops near the craggy rocks on the beach at Guilford Point. We do not speak, comfortable together. The sun sinks over the now placid waters. Sea breezes sigh and gently shift. It is so blessed, so unbelievable, that we have finally found each other.

"André, you do have to tell me now," I finally say. "So many nights I have dreamt of Maman and Madeleine." Tears well up in my eyes and my throat tightens. I cannot speak so I look down at the sand. "If only I had not told Maman to take her little cart... we might have stayed together."

"It was not your fault, Rose." He buries his face in his hands as if he cannot bear it. "Rose, it was the English that caused their death and the deaths of hundreds of Acadians. Oh my god, they had no mercy." He raises his head and looks at me, "You and I were lucky to survive, Rose, but sometimes on that hell ship, I wished to die."

The sea crashes more heavily on the beach now and I have to move beside him to hear him. I look up at him as I used, so often to do. His voice is different now, deeper, and richer, more the voice of a man, not a boy. I smell the sweat in his clothes, see a wrinkle creasing the skin on his broad brow and I accept that we both are older now. I move yet closer for a few moments. The sea wind has risen as if a storm might be brewing. He faces me and takes my hand.

"I need to tell you this," he says. "For I was there and saw the sad things happening. And it is so sad. Little Madeleine wasted away. Her belly threw up the moldy bread and meat with maggots. But we kept feeding her her until one day she took a turn for the better. Rose," he looks at me, "I have cared for her these past years. Madeleine and I are close friends, even family."

"Oh, where is she?" shaking and crying and smiling, I beg for news.

"She is now in my little cabin down the road from Guilford House." He smiles gently, "probably cooking up *petites poutines* to go with the fish I usually bring home."

"Oh, oh, I'm so happy. Alive!" I shriek." Madeleine is alive!" I call to the winds.

"Yes, very much so, Rose," He looks away from me and rubs his eyes, "But your Maman..."

I try to stand firmly on my own but in the chill winds, my body starts to shake. For I know what is coming. Oh god, Maman, Céline, I want you with me. I want to see your brown eyes glowing, saying, *"Allons, ma fille*, let's join the dancing... oh..."* I scream into the blowing wind, "Damn the English, they've killed us all!" and collapse into Andrés arms. He holds me until I stop shaking. "Sist... rest now, dear one. Shall I tell you more?" he asks.

"No, I cannot bear it now, to hear how she suffered. Later, but not now! We must go back. It's near dark and you can tell me as we go, about Madeleine, and when Jacques and I can see her."

"NO. Let me tell you quickly as it was," he says. "Your mother, worn out from caring for Madeleine night and day, weakened and died of smallpox. She was buried at sea."

My shoulders heave with sobs, and he holds me gently against his chest. When I finally stop crying, he lets go of me and straightens up, and says, "And yet there is more."

His face, indeed, looks as if it is frozen, tense with care for me... It is clear now. we both are different now from the way we were when we were promised to each other. We must take our life in our own hands now.

He speaks half to me and half to the sea as he fights to control his feelings. "My mother, passed as well and I mourn her loss."

It is time, past time, for me to reach up to André and hold him as close as I can. Finally, he says, his voice shaking, "Rose, Rose, who knew what life would bring to us."

"André, you were the first one to know my heart. Life has set us on different paths. I struggle to know my way now." Wiping a hand across my tears, I see visions of Nate's broad, honest loving face, of laughing Sarah, of dear baby Caleb smiling a toothless smile at me, of Pegg's shy hidden glance. "But I have known love."

André tenderly takes me in his arms, "And may God's blessing be with them who loved you," he says, and then he drops his arms to his side. We reach out and touch our fingertips before I drop my hand.

"Has Pierre told you, his plans?" he asks.

"He has said that he wants to return to Acadia. We have had little time to talk," I say.

"Pierre and Marie Josèphe hope to find a little patch of rugged land near the coast in Acadia where they can build a house and the English won't bother them. He knows he can work as a fisherman."

"Not a farmer, like Papa?"

André frowns. "We have heard that all the fertile Acadian farmland in Nova Scotia was given to English families."

André sifts sand through his long fingers as he sits facing me on the sand, "Now, what will my favorite, Jacques, choose to do?"

"You know Jacques. He loves his brother and, he admires you, it's so hard for children to face these decisions. But I guess that he will finally want to stay with Pierre and go on to Acadia." My voice drops as my eyes fill with tears, at the thought of losing Jacques, my joy, and life in hard times. He takes my hand, "*un garçon spécial, je pense.*"

We both sit quietly, the losses and deaths of our past sweeping over us.

Knowing it is the time; that we need to find our path though life ahead, I ask him, "Where will you go, Andre?"

"I had planned to leave soon for French territory, the islands of St. Pierre-Miquelon, with Madeleine, and perhaps start a little store like Papa's. I've no wish to live under English rule again. I can visit Papa in Annapolis Royal yearly from there... Still, I'm worried about Madeleine and suggest she go with Pierre. But she weeps and cries and says, that I am nearly her Papa and she wants to stay with me."

He smiles, "How could I know that you would drop out of the sky? Madeleine is a strong-willed little girl. Who knows now what she will want to do? Who she wants to stay with? I'm sure, really, she'll want to stay with you Rose. But then, what will you do? Alone in the middle of America? You know we must all leave the English provinces now."

André looks intently at me and says, "You might like to be with me, Rose, my chosen one. What does your little bird now whisper in your ear?"

He wraps his arms around me as I look outward and ponder and quietly say, "Let's see what Madeleine wishes, André, and of course, my little bird. We must listen to them both, but mostly to you." I turn a little, so he sees my face. I'm smiling.

"Rose, of my heart, we have long been parted and I love you as I always have. Tell me your heart-wish."

"André, for all these years, I've kept you in my heart, loving you, wondering... Now, I know! I wish to be with you as we once dreamed we would be. I love you and I'd like to travel with you and my sister and go on to this island, Miquelon."

A crooked smile creases André's face and pleasure shines in his eyes. "I had forgotten about the little bird, but never about you." We stand, our eyes meet, and we embrace.

The sandflies begin to bite, and we look at each other. "We must get back," André says. "And we have much to talk about."

As I look out at the gathering dusk, words rise to my lips. "Fate has brought us glad hearts," I say softly. We walk back to his horse and wagon. André starts up and we quietly sit together on the wagon bench until he pulls his horse to a stop near The Acadian House.

CHAPTER FORTY-ONE

THE WAY AHEAD

Later, when I stand alone in the clearing near the Acadian House, the evening has just a touch of pink in the sky and Marie Josèphe still works in the garden behind the house. When she sees me, she rushes to meet me. We find a bench to sit on and talk and laugh and cry together as we did for so many years. How good it is to be with her. But I do not tell her about the decision that we have just made. When it is pitch dark, she brings me a candle and guides me to a room where I slip into bed, until the morrow.

The next day, a local man leaves for the New London docks. There, he will look for fishermen who will return to East Hampton with a letter, which I have paid a scribe to write to Nate. I have had the scribe write, "My dear Nate, part of my spirit is always with you. But I go onward. *Au Revoir*, Rose."

The next evening, Pierre, on his return from his day's fishing, greets me with a loud roar of welcome. "C'est bien, Rosalie, you look well and a bit fatter than a few days ago when you came. Are you ready for the journey with me and Marie Josèphe? "

I raise my hand to hold off my answer to his question. He does not know that André and I have talked, for I wanted to face this myself. "Pierre, we must talk."

"Yes, I have planned for the journey." Pierre's brown eyes sparkle as he tells me of the little cradle he has made for their baby. "And besides, I have worked to fill two barrels with dried food to feed us on the way. Marie Josèphe wants to take the little clothes the women made for the infant and that thick wool sweater of the wool of East Hampton sheep that she made for me." He looks at me, "What do you want to bring?"

He does not wait for my words and says, "I'll try and fit in whatever you need. Our sloop is quite large."

Now I take a deep breath. My spirit rises against his sure belief that he always knows what's best for me. His way of acting as if he is in charge has grown even more, since Papa has died. But I have made my own decision. I know now that I must speak out boldly. I alone, now with André, need to follow my path.

"Pierre, I am not coming with you."

"What!" His voice rings out as if I had just disobeyed an order.

"Do not speak to me like that, Pierre," I say and turn away from him.

He stands in front of me again.

Now I stare at him, "My wish is to go with André to the islands, St Pierre Miquelon." I say calmly, although I feel like I stand on a tilting raft amid a stormy ocean.

Pierre stamps his foot and shakes his head. Words pour out of his mouth. "You don't know what you do, Rose, and you will be sorry, mark my words. What about Madeleine? What would Maman and Papa say?"

"Pierre, you know Maman and Papa approved of André. I tell you from my heart that it is a sudden decision for me but now in my heart feels right. André and I have talked. And Madeleine wishes to stay with him. I have to follow my heart, Pierre. You will follow your heart to return to Acadia. Others here may go to Louisiane or France or maybe try to stay here in Guilford. I chose to go on a separate path...."

Pierre still stares at me, and I am uncomfortable with everyone hearing our argument. Staring back at him, I quickly shift my head and gaze towards a spot under a tree away from the group. We walk there and stand alone, the leafy branches surrounding us. The change helps us both to calm ourselves.

"What are your plans, then, Rose?" he says quietly.

I tell him of my meeting with André and Madeleine's wish to go with him.

"Pierre, this is our life, André and I loved each other when we were in Acadia, and we do today. Papa and Maman will bless us, I know," I reach up to him and try to reach his broad chest. "You are a bigger man now!" I chuckle.

"Our plans are just starting, but we will work together, just as you will with Marie Josèphe...

"We yet have to plan how to get to the islands. But once there, I may help André by perhaps helping him start a little spot to sell Acadian food in Miquelon and Madeleine can help."

I choke back tears when joy and sadness overwhelm me.

A soft evening mist drifts over us when finally, he says, "Rose, until the very last moment, I will hold my hope that you come with us. Change your mind, if you can." He speaks softly, now. A little group of Acadians is still watching us. They look at me kindly.

Smiling a little, I look at Pierre and gently shake my head. "*Bon voyage, mon frère.* May you have a safe journey to Acadia." I stand tall and look him in the eyes.

"Perhaps André will work our passage to New York by signing on as seaman or working on a fishing boat out of New London. From New York, we hope we can get on to St. Pierre the same way. Somehow, Madeleine and I will get aboard, maybe I can cook for the voyage."

Pierre speaks in a solemn voice. "Rose, it's your life and I will not stand in your way. My blessings are with you. We will miss you, dear Rose. I pray that we will meet again."

The stern set of Pierre's face softens as he says this and, in this moment, he looks like Papa, with Papa's sweet smile. His eyes are kind now.

My eyes meet Pierre's. I step forward and throw my arms around him. "*Merci, mon frère.*"

Jacques again runs up to stand by his big brother. He has always loved to be with him. Pierre stands speechless for a moment, looking at the sun setting in an orange sky layered around with deep blue clouds. Shaking his head, he walks off to join Marie Josèphe. Jacques follows him. They talk to a quiet group of Acadians near the Acadian House. I talk to a few women who come to bid me good night, and then I slip past them to the little room where I spent last night.

Pierre and I talk in the next day about memories of our family. I tell him a few things about his brother, grown older now, that he might not know.

Two days later, Pierre, Marie Josèphe and Jacques are picked up by a wagon with their things. They go to board the sloop that will take them through New York Harbor and far up the Hudson River to the point where they must leave the boat behind and set out on their own across the forests of northern New York. Even when they reach Canada, their journey will be long.

Now, it is done, the searing thought stabs me again that I may never see Pierre or Jacques again. But it gives me strength to know that this hard loss is one that I chose myself, alone, not one that was forced on me.

Now that Pierre and the others have left, I will be all alone with my Acadians but not my very own family. As my mind spins about, worrying about my family and me, and what to do, tears flood my eyes. I am like a single star among the scattered stars of Acadians who wander the world.

And since my family is not here to help me explain, it makes it harder for me. One old woman says, "prepare for the bad days, my child." I go to her, kneel and take her hand in my hand and say, "*Oui*, please bless us for the good days and the bad." She raises her hand and blesses us with a sign of the cross and we clutch hands together.

All is so different now for us Acadians. She has lost her son, and I have lost my parents, but God is there, and we pray for His guidance in our life to come. The people bring out beer and the men talk with André about what we might find in St. Pierre-Miquelon.

It is not so comfortable for any of us, so André does not stay the night but goes back to his boat to sleep. Before he leaves, I pull his head down so I can whisper good night, to him. And he is off with a steady gait to the beach, to get his boat ready, he says.

When the morning comes and André arrives, one of the old men asks if we would accept a blessing from him and all the Acadians.

"With thanks," André says calmly. So that afternoon, we stand with bowed heads together in front of a little group of Acadians under the trees near The Acadian House. The elder makes the Sign of the Cross over us and then says solemnly, "In the name of the Lord, may you be steady through happiness and sadness, may you live long, have many children and peace at the end. Amen."

There is silence and then a burst of fiddle music, and André and I and Madeline smile and hug. Then we share in a little feast my Acadians have scraped together. A couple does a few dance steps, and an old granny gives me her shawl, washed and aged as it is, "to remember the ancients," she says with a toothless grin. We share in laughter and tears.

Finally, night falls over us, and we say bonne nuit to all. André says and returns to the cottage as I fall into bed in The Acadian House.

Very early the next day, I wake, dress and see him outside with Madeleine, and I know it is time. He greets me with a kiss and takes my little trunk and other things and we slip away knowing I will never see these dear Acadians again. And again, I cry: for the past, not the future.

On the sloop, the captain, André's friend, knowing the waters and tides, sails his sloop without peril through the bay and on to piers of the Port of New York, where we bid the captain farewell and thanks.

Into my heart floods a breath-taking time of hope. André takes my hand and Madeleine, André, and I climb from the wobbly deck of the sloop to the pier. He puts his arm around my shoulder as the captain unloads our few goods, and we look for a ship for him to sign on a seaman for the trip to the islands of Saint Pierre and Miquelon.

We know that we face a new life. But we know that our new land, St Pierre-Miquelon has for years welcomed people from different countries. Whatever lies ahead, with great joy, together, we start a new life.

AUTHOR'S NOTE

This is a work of historical fiction. Early East Hampton town records and other sources document that an Acadian family was placed in East Hampton, New York, just before the French and Indian War was declared in America. Many people in East Hampton were kind to that family.

Master Jonas is a creation: and he had a grudge against anything French because his son had been wounded by the French. Indeed, some other English people in New York suspected that the Acadians were spies or enemies. And so, in this story, Rose was a victim of prejudice, at least for a time.

The plot and characters in this story arise only from the author's imagination.

ABOUT THE AUTHOR

Sheila Flynn DeCosse picked up a pen in grade school and has been at it ever since. She has published non-fiction articles, adult and children's fiction and poetry.

All of her grandparents were immigrants from Ireland and Wales to New York City. She has always been interested in tales of immigration to America. When she became aware of the placement of refugee Acadians in Colonial East Hampton, New York, her interest was aroused.

The tragedy of the English exile of a complete population from Acadia to America in the early years of the French and Indian War was not known to her or to many. She thought the story was one that deserved to be told.

For some immigrants, as in this story, the challenge of learning a new language is difficult. But learning a new language can help open a new path to life.

Sheila received her BA in English from Manhattanville College and a MA in Library Science from the University of Wisconsin-Milwaukee. She has participated in numerous creative writing programs and is a member of The Society of Children's Book Writers and Illustrators

ABOUT TBR BOOKS

a program of CALEC

TBR Books is a program of the Center for the Advancement of Languages, Education, and Communities. We publish researchers and practitioners who seek to engage diverse communities on topics related to education, languages, cultural history, and social initiatives. We translate our books in a variety of languages to further expand our impact. Become a member of TBR Books and receive complimentary access to all our books.

Our Books in English

Rose Alone by Sheila Flynn DeCosse

Immigrant Dreams: A Memoir by Barbara Goldowsky

Salsa Dancing in Gym Shoes: Developing Cultural Competence to Foster Latino Student Success by Tammy Oberg de la Garza and Alyson Leah Lavigne

Mamma in her Village by Maristella de Panniza Lorch

The Other Shore by Maristella de Panniza Lorch

The Clarks of Willsborough Point: A Journey through Childhood by Darcey Hale

Beyond Gibraltar by Maristella de Panniza Lorch

The Gift of Languages: Paradigm Shift in U.S. Foreign Language Education by Fabrice Jaumont and Kathleen Stein-Smith

Two Centuries of French Education in New York: The Role of Schools in Cultural Diplomacy by Jane Flatau Ross

The Clarks of Willsborough Point: The Long Trek North by Darcey Hale

The Bilingual Revolution: The Future of Education is in Two Languages by Fabrice Jaumont

Our Books in Translation

La Rivoluzione bilingue: Il futuro dell'istruzione in due lingue by Fabrice Jaumont

El regalo de las lenguas : Un cambio de paradigma en la enseñanza de las lenguas extranjeras en Estados Unidos de Fabrice Jaumont y Kathleen Stein-Smith

Rewolucja Dwujęzyczna: Przyszłość edukacji jest w dwóch językach by Fabrice Jaumont

Le don des langues : *vers un changement de paradigme dans l'enseignement des langues étrangères aux États-Unis* de Fabrice Jaumont et Kathleen Stein-Smith

Our books are available on our website and on all major online bookstores as paperback and e-book. Some of our books have been translated in Arabic, Chinese, English, French, German, Italian, Japanese, Polish, Russian, Spanish. For a listing of all books published by TBR Books, information on our series, or for our submission guidelines for authors, visit our website at

www.tbr-books.org

ABOUT CALEC

The Center for the Advancement of Languages, Education, and Communities (CALEC) is a nonprofit organization focused on promoting multilingualism, empowering multilingual families, and fostering cross-cultural understanding. The Center's mission is in alignment with the United Nations' Sustainable Development Goals. Our mission is to establish language as a critical life skill, through developing and implementing bilingual education programs, promoting diversity, reducing inequality, and helping to provide quality education. Our programs seek to protect world cultural heritage and support teachers, authors, and families by providing the knowledge and resources to create vibrant multilingual communities.

The specific objectives and purpose of our organization are:

To develop and implement education programs that promote multilingualism and cross-cultural understanding, and establish an inclusive and equitable quality education, including internship and leadership training. [SDG # 4, Quality Education]

To publish and distribute resources, including research papers, books, and case studies that seek to empower and promote the social, economic and political inclusion of all, with a focus on language education and cultural diversity, equity and inclusion. [SDG # 10, Reduced Inequalities]

To help build sustainable cities and communities and support teachers, authors, researchers, and families in the advancement of multilingualism and cross-cultural understanding through collaborative tools for linguistic communities. [SDG # 11, Sustainable Cities and Communities]

To foster strong global partnerships and cooperation, and mobilize resources across borders, to participate in events and activities that promote language education through knowledge sharing and coaching, empowering parents and teachers, and building multilingual societies. [SDG # 17, Partnerships for the Goals]

Support Our Mission

The Center for the Advancement of Languages, Education, and Communities (CALEC) is a public charity exempt from federal income tax under Internal Revenue Code (IRC) Section 501(c) (3).

www.calec.org

9 781636 071664